HOW she came to be enveloped in his arms was something Sharonne would never know. Her heart pounded and the blood swirled so madly in her veins that she was unable to protest—had she even wished to. All she was suddenly aware of was his eyes, firing, burning into her very soul.

"Sharonne, I find you a challenge."

"Stop! No . . . please . . . Edmund . . . , " she tried to protest but failed lamentably.

"If you would stop me, why do you cling to me so avidly?" he parried, his lips unrelenting.

"Ed . . . mund . . . , " she gasped, floundering in a sea of delirium. "We have not been acquainted . . . one hour. . . . "

"How long would you have? How long does it take to acknowledge the inevitable?"

COUNTER-PARRY

A Novel by

Freda Michel

FAWCETT CREST • NEW YORK

COUNTER-PARRY

THIS BOOK CONTAINS THE COMPLETE TEXT OF
THE ORIGINAL HARDCOVER EDITION.

Published by Fawcett Crest Books, a unit of CBS Publications, the Consumer Publishing Division of CBS Inc., by arrangement with Robert Hale Limited

ISBN: 0-449-23842-3

Printed in the United States of America

10 9 8 7 6 5 4 3 2 1

PART ONE

1

A GIRLISH giggle rippled over the sweet tranquillity of London's Hyde Park as it basked in the moonlight of a late spring eve—swiftly dogged by a scuffle and rustle of silks, bringing an adjacent laurel bush to sudden, somewhat violent, animation.

"Fie on you, impetuous sir," mildly admonished the female, her tinkling voice lacking conviction, nonetheless. "Dost thou think I dispense my kisses as freely as a tree doth its leaves in an autumn wind?"

"Egad, nay, ma'am—er—Miss L-Lingfield . . . H-Hen . . . rie . . . tta . . . m-my love . . . my life!" gasped the lovelorn youth, as if about to expire with desire on the spot. "I—I swear 'fore heaven, your kisses are more precious to me than all the gems in Christendom! More than the very stars up yonder! Forsooth, I live only for you, joy o' my heart—for the touch o' your soft white hand . . . the nectar o' your lips . . . the gentle caress o' your—"

"'S blood! Unhand my sister this instant, you impudent scoundrel!" bellowed an unexpected voice of the masculine gender at this point as the thunder of feet—evidently supporting a figure of substantial proportions—bore down upon the tender scene, creating prodigious uproar. "Y-You lecherous young jackanapes! By Satan, I'll teach you to lay your filthy whore-mongering hands upon my sister—"

"Sir! My lord! I protest!" besought the youth to little avail.

"No, Richard! No!" cried my lady, her entreaty culminating in a piercing scream as a resounding smack silenced her swain.

And following a miscellany of thumps, grunts and shrieks, a human cannon-ball shot out from behind the laurel in a flurry of blue satin and white lace, red heels cartwheeling over fashionably powdered head, to land with a jarring thud amongst the nearby undergrowth.

An outraged visage, defying all description, then protruded round the aforesaid bush to fling a final blistering oath after the unfortunate Lothario, before the owner seized the distrait maiden's arm and dragged her away from the abortive rendezvous in the opposite direction, their high heels tapping indignantly into obscurity.

All was silent again upon the balmy night air, prompting the overhead nightingale to overture a few tentative notes to ascertain if the atmosphere were now conducive to the resumption of her song. But the only discordant sound to be heard was of the muttered curses emanating from the prostrate youth who was endeavouring to extricate himself from a rather prickly thicket.

This accomplished, he then dubiously probed his person to determine the full extent of his injuries, the worst chancing to be his left eye which was swelling at an alarming rate, though not nearly so painful as the injury borne by his dignity. Once assured that nothing was broken, the youth staggered to his feet to dust himself down and shake out the crumpled Flanders lace beneath his scratched chin, whilst dabbing intermittently at his offending eye with lace-trimmed handkerchief. Finally retrieving his silver-laced cocked hat, he knocked it savagely into shape, rammed it on his head, squared his young virile shoulders and lurched off in search of the nearest ale-house, grumbling and cursing as he went, and kicking furiously at anything foolish enough to come within range of his elegantly-shod feet.

Jonathan Falconer was no exception to other young bucks of the day who, at the tender age of nineteen summers, made the imprudent error of allowing their passion to ride roughshod over their sense of reason, forcing their attentions—though not entirely unsolicited—upon the lady of their heart's desire, with the same tragic result.

Even as he brooded thus in sullen resentment, one hand tenderly caressing his nether regions, Jonathan was quite unaware that he had already quitted the park and was involuntarily following whither his feet would lead, namely, to St James's Street where was situated White's, the most fashionable and exclusive gentleman's club in English Society, and of which the youth was eminently proud to boast he had recently been enrolled a member.

Upon arrival at this unparagoned establishment he paused to consider his appearance which, he was relieved to find, was all it should be—barring his unfortunate optic—for despite his harrowing experience, his coat of blue satin and silver lace, styled in the height of ton (and costing his father a tolerable sum) had emerged unscathed, proclaiming him a gentleman of consequence, not to mention the gleaming gold-hilted dress-sword by his side which he clutched feverishly the while, as if eager to put it to use.

Thus, with arrogant, almost insolent, air he mounted the steps and entered the hallowed portals, to have his ego somewhat deflated by an anxious enquiry into the cause of his blackened eye. Jonathan managed to stammer some weak excuse about colliding with a statue in the park which the porter seemed ready to accept as he bowed respectfully, expressing a relief that the young sir had not been attacked by footpads, alas, an all too frequent occurrence. Overcoming an impulse to advise the fellow to heed his own damned business, Jonathan merely scowled thunderously whilst delivering his hat into the other's charge.

Without further annoyance he proceeded to the gaming salon, thankful to note that it was well attended upon this particular night, enabling him to mingle virtually unnoticed, for he wished to evade attention—not only on account of his eye and the embarrassing questions it might evoke, but because he had a deal to ruminate and so cherished little inclination for conversation. To his satisfaction, he was able to seat himself out of prominent sight in a remote corner of the room where he was at liberty to submerge his troubles in a variety of intoxicants without any interference. And although, understandably, one or two curious glances were cast his way, his eye occasioned no further remark.

Once established, he thirstily consumed three glasses of Madeira before allowing his inquisitive gaze to travel round the salon, his curiosity overcoming his reluctance to spy a familiar face. Howbeit, none but a friend of the stoutest heart would have felt inclined to approach Jonathan, for his ill-humour and disfigured countenance rendered his customary plain but pleasing looks most forbidding.

Through his thick sandy-coloured brows he furtively surveyed the distinguished gathering besporting themselves at the tables, frittering away their inheritances with nonchalant abandon 'neath the beatific effects of inebriation and the incessant prattle of lively repartee, all seeking to relieve their boredom or straitened circumstances across the green baize upon which stakes of priceless gems, golden guineas, seals and snuff-boxes winked and flashed in the brilliance of the chandeliers suspended overhead.

Thus, the room buzzed with commotion, but at a table not far from Jonathan languished a group of exquisites apparently seeking to win some prize for creating the most disturbance, evoking looks of abject scorn, irritation—even hatred and unmitigated anger—yet to whom not a solitary soul present seemed willing to overture a word of censure. As if abundantly aware of this, the group continued gaming and carousing in reckless style, jingling their guineas, bottles and glasses to a catenation of toe-curling bawdy jokes, back-slapping and raucous laughter.

Ere long, Jonathan too became irritated by the din which did little to alleviate his wretchedness, as with each sip of wine he mentally relived his harrowing indignity in the park. Nevertheless, he was prepared to endure it along with everyone else—though by no means on account of cowardice, for the gentlemen concerned were all utter strangers to him. No, he was still extremely loath to attract attention and shrank deeper into his shell of reserve, consuming glass upon glass of wine whilst cursing to perdition every member of the female sex. However, seated in such proximity to the jovial band Jonathan could not prevent snatches of their conversation encroaching upon his thoughts.

"Plague take ye, Rave!" one modish member was rebuking another in highly cultured tone. "Ye've dealt me flat hands all eve. Let Froth ha' the cards."

"Froth!" ejaculated the other with incredulous laugh.

"Aye, damme—hic—why not?" declared the outlandish fop with his back to Jonathan, evidently the indignant (and somewhat inebriated) 'Froth'. "S-Stap me vitals—hic—could scarce do worse, eh, Gabe?"

"Even if you are three parts under the table," yawned the devastating exquisite half-facing Jonathan, his inordinate length draped across two chairs and best part of a third whilst his immaculate head and shoulders lay propped against 'Rave' who, though perched upon a mere hair's breadth of space, seemed quite impervious to the discomfort.

It may have been the audacious inflection in the well-modulated voice which drew Jonathan's eyes to the inanimate owner, upon whom they remained transfixed in surprise, awe and curiosity, not intending to stare so brazenly yet unable to drag his eyes away. Suddenly the most consummate jealousy welled up in him at sight of this stranger whose every glance, gesture, exuded the self-confidence that Jonathan craved—but never more than at that precise moment after suffering such gross insult at the hands of his inamorata's noxious brother.

If the arrogant gentleman observed Jonathan's unabashed malignant gaze he certainly gave no indication of it as he played his cards with a practised hand, for he was well accustomed to the wide-eyed interest his person engendered and should have suspected something dreadfully amiss had he failed so to do—likewise, the passionate feeling he generated in the youthful heart, love or hatred, male or female, he could tolerate all—

except indifference which, he was content to note, he had never yet encountered.

This was hardly surprising for never was man more open contradiction of himself. Indeed, he was so fair and delicately featured one might have assumed him to be a lady incognito. Blond silken hair, unpowdered and lightly confined in a stiff black bow, showered like quicksilver down his back, with wanton curls framing a face pre-eminently beautiful despite his gender, pale and classically handsome as if cast in the mould of some Grecian god. Even his physique, in defiance of his goodly height, would seem a trifle slender and boyish beneath the cream brocade and gold lace for one of his nine-and-twenty years. All, in fact, testifying that Mother Nature had intended him to be female but, no less capricious than the rest of her sex, had changed her mind, and in her eagerness to redeem him from the jaws of such fate had lavished upon him physical strength, emotions and desires so overwhelmingly masculine as to give the lie to his effeminate façade. With such highly developed masculine weaknesses he had rapidly galloped downhill to the very devil and although his angelic looks proclaimed him a child of God, upon his soul was branded for all time the cloven hoof of Satan for within him his infernal master had kindled an insatiable fiendish appetite which he sought constantly to appease with new and more novel atrocities—each more novel and atrocious than the last—no matter what the cost to others as long as it relieved the intolerable boredom which invariably shrouded him.

Jonathan forced his eyes away, more incensed with himself at allowing the stranger to affect him so, and took succour in another glass of wine, striving to focus his thoughts upon his problem upon which he had managed to concentrate without any difficulty a short while since.

But the fair exquisite's inane laughter continued to obtrude upon his meditations, refusing to let his anger die, goading him more and more until he could cheerfully have whipped forth his sword and riveted the man to one of his three chairs, though why he could not say . . . as yet.

"May m' soul rot in hell, Gabe," averred the bag-wigged spark in emerald satin, crossing himself in mock piety, "if I speak the breath of a lie."

" 'Tis like to rot either way, my friend," returned his languid companion, availing himself of a generous pinch of snuff from someone else's box.

"As heaven's my witness! Called out at crack o' dawn, I was, and run through the ribs—"

"Because of an accurst shoe?" cried Rave in astonishment.

"Aye, I flung it into a ditch."

"And he took violent exception?" pressed another member with interest.

"Forsooth, for I do believe his foot was in't at the time."

A gale of laughter went up, inspiring the fair Gabe to relate a similar incident, quite oblivious to the hostility building up in the club's newest patron.

"Faith, I vow I encountered like injustice when I collided with some blackguardly fellow's sister during the dance," he drawled, his companions gathering closer, agog.

"B' gad! Not the ravishing Cyprian I spied ye seducin' in Spring Gardens last Friday's eve?" questioned the highly cultured voice, rising two tones in pitch.

"The same, m' dear Ross, though, alas, the name eludes me. I collided with the wench headlong, or rather b———" The discreetly murmured word, whatever it was, evoked a burst of hysteria, ere he resumed, "For, rot me if I did not contact—somewhat vigorously, I confess—that vulnerable though exceeding well-upholstered part of her anatomy from whence I did rebound half-way down the room."

The group rocked with laughter at the picture though the narrator maintained an expression of placid indifference as he idly wafted grains of snuff from one huge bejewelled cuff.

" 'Pon rep, Gabe!" gasped Ross, dabbing painstakingly at his streaming eyes with jasmine-impregnated handkerchief. "Devil take me if I shouldn't mind rebounding' off the said damsel meself."

The other's cynical lips curled slowly, as if the recollection did not entirely displease him.

"Aye," he accorded wistfully. "I'll own the encounter had its compensations . . . was't Longwood? Or Langford? Nay—'twas Lingfield."

Lingfield! Jonathan bolted upright at the name, almost upsetting the bottles at his elbow as his heart leapt to the beat of a war-drum. No, not *his* Lingfield? Surely these scoundrels did not presume to slander, revile the name of the sweetest creature on earth, his dearest adorable Henrietta? The one for whom he had languished and pined over the past weeks until he had finally summoned sufficient courage to declare himself that very evening with such disastrous consequences?

His beloved one, whose name only the saints in heaven were worthy of breathing—not these lecherous dogs!

The vision of this beautiful blond reprobate laying hands upon his peerless love, defiling her innocence, turned Jonathan's brain into a blazing inferno of hatred, and without a second's hesitation he stormed across to confront the one responsible for the outrage, his slight though lissome frame trembling in fury as he drew himself up to his full five feet four inches.

"Sirrah! You heinously malign the good name of a lady for whom I hold the highest regard—for which I demand—"

Jonathan got no further, for his arm was seized from behind and he was dragged bodily aside. Surprise was dogged swiftly by wildest indignation as he rounded on the intruder who presumed to lay hands upon him, and found himself staring up into an elderly face, drawn with anxiety.

"You young hot-head! Have you lost your wits, boy?" exclaimed the gentleman, aghast.

"No, sir!" rejoined Jonathan, taking wrathful exception to the other's tone and presumption, struggling to free himself. "I would merely see justice done. And I'll thank you to let go of me, whoever you are!"

"Which is all very admirable," went on the man, gripping Jonathan's arm the tighter. "But do you realise whom you were addressing in such hostile manner?"

"I was addressing yonder coxcomb!"

"Coxcomb!" ejaculated the gentleman, involuntarily drawing the youth three paces further away as he glanced furtively round, hoping no one had overhead. "Impetuous youth! Guard your tongue, the very walls can hear. You are evidently not aware that the personage you so recklessly slander happens to be none other than Lord Ashton!"

"Ashton?" queried Jonathan, the name conveying nothing.

"Gabriel St Claire, Marquess of Ashton," clarified the man, making Jonathan little wiser. "Obviously you know nought of the man or his vile repute or you would not stand here bandying words with me. Take warning, young sir, he is not to be trifled with. I suggest you leave as unobtrusively as possible and head homewards without delay, giving thanks to heaven that by some miracle your hasty words passed unheard."

This set-down added fuel to Jonathan's fire of indignation, and wrenching his arm free he turned angrily upon the gentleman.

"I thank you, sir, for your kind concern, but I assure you I have fought more duels than I care to number, and am well able to take care of myself!"

The old gentleman stepped back as if he had been struck across his benevolent face, and his manner changed.

"I apologise most humbly for taking so much upon myself," he replied in offended tone—suddenly drawing himself up with a surge of pride. "Even so, you would do well to beware of the Ashton set." And with a curt bow he disappeared into the crowd.

An ungovernable fury broke loose in Jonathan, and with smoke virtually belching from his nostrils he charged straight for the Marquess whom he held entirely responsible for his present wretched plight. All was finished! After his bitter humiliation in Hyde Park his fair Henrietta would never speak to him again, which would make his existence unbearable. There was

16

nothing now to live for, so he would die, if needs be, defending her honour!

"Sir!" he shouted as loud as he could above the din, stomping to a halt by the Marquess's chairs. "I demand immediate satisfaction!"

This did not evoke the sudden dramatic reaction anticipated, but the fact that the noise gradually dwindled to a murmur and the intoxicated Froth was striving against overpowering odds to focus his dilating orbs upon him seemed proof enough that his words had been heard—though the Marquess himself gave not the slightest intimation of it, until he spoke.

"Doth mine ears deceive me, Rave, or did I perchance hear an alien sound?"

It was the Honourable Benjamin Fotheringham who now drew his lordship's attention to the irate Jonathan standing at his side, prepared to do battle with hand ominously clenched upon sword hilt.

" 'Sh blood, Gabe—hic—b-but I do b'lieve . . . 'twash thish black-eyed—hic—sh-shtriplin'!"

"Stripling?" enquired my lord with interest, anticipating some new diversion at someone else's expense. " 'Pon my life, so there is. Well, well, gentlemen, what do we have here?"

Jonathan shuffled uncomfortably from foot to foot as the jolly band perused him from bruised visage to muddy shoes in varying degrees of amusement.

"Can't be certain," submitted Lord Ravenby dubiously, "but thought I heard the fellow demanding something."

"Satisfaction!" supplied Viscount Ross, aggravating the fomenting situation in eager expectation of some riotous sport. "Marches up to Gabe here, an' demands

satisfaction as cool as ye please. Curse me—ha! ha! ha!
—if 'tan't the wildest thing since Swindley raced that
bull at Newmarket, eh, Ravenby?"

Lord Ravenby returned the vestige of a smile, being
the only member of the party to boast anything resem-
bling a conscience, and glanced warily betwixt his
friend the Marquess and Jonathan, as if trying to esti-
mate how the emotional current was to flow.

Meanwhile, the Marquess's eyes—of the hardest and
most frigid ice-blue Jonathan had ever seen—rested
contemptuously upon his newly acquired foe.

"Well, stripling?" he purred in indolent amusement.
"Did you indeed challenge me?"

Jonathan could only nod as he unexpectedly laboured 'neath severe constriction of the throat.

"So, you've challenged me," my lord shrugged with
casual indifference. "You may go claim your prize and
redeem your stake."

"It is not a wager!" bristled the youth.

"No? Er—a jest, perhaps? Though I must confess I
find your sense of humour even more perverted than
mine."

The laughter was cut short by Lord Ravenby, who
was anxious to terminate the little interlude before it
should turn sour.

"All right, stripling, you've had your fun. Now take
yourself off, there's a good fellow."

This did the trick and the group turned back to resume the game, despatching Jonathan from their minds.

But Jonathan refused to be thus dismissed like some
troublesome lackey! And to prove his point, again
voiced his demands whilst giving the table vigorous
thumps, setting guineas and glasses jumping and jan-

gling in rhythm, inducing irate cries from those assembled.

"Gadswoons! Desist, ye clumsy oaf! Hell and the devil!"—came the chorus of protest.

"Satan's death!" declared Lord Ross above everyone else. "Give him satisfaction, Gabe!"

"Aye, run the squint-eyed puppy through!" abetted another.

Despite his reputation, it would seem upon this particular night that Lord Ashton was not to be easily provoked. Indeed, Lord Ravenby cherished nought but profound admiration for his friend's extreme tolerance of the drunken youth who did not appear to appreciate the miraculous reprieve he was being granted and that he might well have been already skewered firmly to the nearest wall by Lord Ashton's deadly rapier had he chanced to find my lord in less amiable humour.

Again the Marquess's cold gaze calmly surveyed Jonathan, in greater detail this time, noting the facial features one by one as if half expecting something to ring familiar, endeavouring to establish a reason for this unprecedented demand, for no one so woefully inexperienced had ever dared challenge him before.

"Stripling, you begin to bore me," he sighed with ennui. "If I am supposed to recall your countenance from the archives of my distant past, I assure you—"

"I am Jonathan Willoughby Falconer," retorted Jonathan, puffing out his under-developed chest. "Son of Sir Giles Falconer of—" He pulled up short, realising the folly of confiding so much to this unscrupulous rake.

"Well?" prompted the other with languid disdain. "Should that imply something?"

Jonathan bit his lip in annoyance, and repeated his challenge parrot-fashion.

"I demand satisfaction, or an instant apology! And I refuse to—"

"For what, an I make s' bold?"

"For what!" echoed Jonathan in amazement. "Sir! You did grossly insult the good name of a lady I esteem most highly!"

The Marquess threw back his head and gave licence to his inane laugh. " 'Twould seem by your appearance that insults to your light o' love are a fairly common occurrence."

Everyone chortled, inducing Jonathan to raise a self-conscious hand to his injured optic as he seethed with further humiliation, aggravated by the knowledge that play had dwindled to a halt throughout the salon and he was now the prime object of attention.

"Your offensiveness is not to be endured, sirrah!" he attacked the Marquess anew. "Lips such as thine are not worthy to speak her name! I must insist you give me satisfaction!"

"Take care, stripling," warned the Marquess, his facetious veneer finally wearing thin and his true colours beginning to emerge, "lest you try my patience too far. Go seek your satisfaction elsewhere."

"Y-You refuse my challenge?" gasped Jonathan, taken aback. "On what grounds?"

"On the grounds that I do not grant satisfaction to every insolent cur who demands it," flung back Lord Ashton witheringly. "Nor do I cross swords with unbreeched babes. I therefore advise you to take your accurst self out of my sight before I make you the exception."

20

"B-But you can't refuse!" Jonathan protested furiously, aware that every eye in the room was riveted on him and that he was becoming a laughing-stock. "Mine honour is at stake! It's against the code!"

"Code?" parried my lord dangerously, slowly lowering his fashionable feet to the floor and sitting up to pierce the youth with a menacing eye, drawing all interested parties closer, feverishly agog lest they miss a single word. "Hear this, my quarrelsome cavalier! Gabriel St Claire honours no man's code but his own. *I* am master of my destiny! *I* make the demands! *I* issue the challenges—when I feel inclined. Consider yourself extremely fortunate, stripling, for tonight I do not feel inclined—a rare occurrence. We are utter strangers, I think? I see before me an immature youth who is unaccustomed to strong liquor and with whom I have no grievance. Go home, and give thanks to the god you worship that I have deigned to spare your miserable hide."

The silence was excruciating as all and sundry waited with bated breath for the youth to collapse, grovelling, at the Marquess's feet, where countless numbers had grovelled before and no doubt would again, paying—in this instance—dutiful homage to his infinite clemency. This Jonathan could not do! Furthermore, the fact that the Marquess openly refused to fight seemed to imply that he was nothing more than the cowardly namby-pamby popinjay he appeared. He was afraid! Afraid of him, Jonathan Falconer! Well, *he* was not afraid to stand up for what he believed to be right! He was no coward, as he would very soon prove to those whispering and tittering behind, by turning the tables on my Lord Marquess and exposing him for what he was.

"So!" he cried with derisive laugh. "This is the renowned Marquess of Ashton, bold leader of the notorious Ashton set! Who sends men, women and children scurrying in fear of their lives! This craven who hasn't the spunk to stand up and defend himself when challenged to his face!" And he rounded off the declaration by snatching up a glass of wine and dashing the contents full in the Marquess's face.

A gasp of horror reverberated round the room.

"Now will you fight, coward?" Jonathan's slurred speech rang out in the tense hushed atmosphere, as the stunned onlookers waited to witness the reaction to this supreme insult, and Jonathan drew his sword with a rasp of steel to stand, muscles taut, ready for the onslaught.

"Let me finish him, Gabe!" cried one exquisite, leaping up, his weapon half-drawn—to be arrested by a gesture from my Lord Marquess.

"By death! The boy must be crazed," exclaimed Lord Ravenby.

" 'Tis downright suicide!" supported another, whilst others called the odds, offering wagers concerning the outcome which seemed so pitifully obvious, no takers were forthcoming.

All eyes were adhered to the Marquess who wiped his face with meticulous care, put away his silk handkerchief, then rose to his feet with agonising deliberation, his pallid countenance utterly inscrutable except for his eyes which glittered like icicles in winter sunshine, searing a hole through Jonathan. However, when he finally spoke his voice was perfectly tranquil.

"Sheath your sword, stripling. I do not indulge in clubhouse brawls."

22

The youth hesitated, suspecting some trick, then did as he asked.

"You appreciate, I trust, that your doom is now sealed?" went on the Marquess, his menacing voice barely a murmur, inducing his rapt audience to cock their ears a trifle more to catch his words. "In truth, if you stood poised upon the scaffold with the rope about your neck, your worthless life would not be more surely forfeit than at this moment. Why you should choose to goad me thus is something betwixt you and your Maker. Many will no doubt witness"—he gestured briefly round the sea of eager faces—"that for once 'twas not of my seeking. Lord Ravenby, here, will act for me." The gentleman stepped forward and bowed gravely in acknowledgment as the Marquess flung a card on the table. "Here is my direction. Kindly furnish him with yours and he will call upon you at noon to-morrow."

Jonathan's blurred vision travelled round the jostling distinguished members, none of whom seemed ready to proffer their services on his behalf, and be party to the slaughter, leaving him with no alternative but to divulge the necessary information.

"Albemarle Street, number nine," he muttered gruffly, his befuddled mind not really crediting that the Marquess intended keeping the appointment. Yes, granted, he was going through the motions of doing so to satisfy the curious, but when it came to the actual fight he would turn tail and run like the timid rabbit he was.

As everything had been said that needed to be, there seemed little else to do but adjourn with as much dignity as he could muster, and so, with a click of heels and stiff bow Jonathan was about retreat when he found himself forcibly detained by the limp ruffles at his throat which were somehow confined in the rigorous grasp of his adversary, compelling him to stare up, up, into a face diabolic beyond belief! So fiendishly distorted with evil intent that Jonathan's brain cleared on the instant and for the first time he experienced something very akin to fear, the nearest he had been all evening to appreciating his predicament, and the true character of the man whose path he had chosen to cross. He blenched, wondering what on earth had possessed him to acknowledge this satanic being, angelic!

"One thing further, stripling," snarled the Marquess, loud enough for all to hear, "—and mark me well. You have finally succeeded in rousing my anger, for which you must pay the price, and make no mistake, my swaggering bantam, you will pay dearly. Enjoy your brief respite, for when next we meet I shall take savage delight in carving your miserable carcass up for the crows! You will learn to your bitter cost how Lord Ashton deals with cock o' the midden braggarts foolish enough to cross him." Adding as he pushed Jonathan roughly away: "Now get out of my sight ere I spit you where you stand!"

Jonathan stumbled but managed to maintain his balance, and turning on his heel quitted the club without as much as a backward glance.

2

DURING his weary trudge back to Albemarle Street, the night air coupled with a light shower of rain served to cool Jonathan's fevered brow and bring him almost to the point of sobriety. And at three in the morning he lay prone upon his bed, tossing and turning in his endeavours to capture the rest and comforting oblivion he desperately craved, yet which anguish and despair constantly sought to deny him, wondering why his whole world had suddenly capsized? Why Fate had cruelly guided his feet to White's on this particular night, and this Lord Ashton's also? But most of all, why the very sight of the man had rankled him so unreasonably, long ere Henrietta's name had been mentioned?

Although his head ached abominably and his stomach heaved in violent protest at the very concept of food, Jonathan presented himself punctually at the breakfast table next morning, primarily to humour his father's strict adherence to punctuality, for he had several rather pertinent questions to put before his sire and therefore wished to promote a genial atmosphere. Appreciably, the utmost discretion would be called for as he had no desire for anyone—least of all his father—to discern his motive. It was imperative that no one should suspect an inkling of the truth!

Around the well-laden table sat arrayed the Falconer family, each absorbed in breaking their fast in their own peculiar manner with the exception of Jonathan who, whilst making a bold attempt to eat, brooded the while, casting sullen looks round the table at the other members present: the portly figure of Sir Giles, dutifully established at the head of the table, humming and hawing betwixt mouthfuls as was his wont, and bestowing commiserating pats upon his full-blown abdomen as each belch erupted with clockwork regularity, whilst Lady Falconer held sway opposite, tall and willowy like a poplar tree and every whit as thin, to whom—contrary to her spouse—meals were a solemn ritual, during which her skeleton-like hands fluttered perpetually with short nervous gestures, as if eager to seize upon some item of food yet unable to decide precisely what; and last of all, but by no means to be ignored, there sat Sharonne, Jonathan's young sister, a wayward minx of some sixteen summers who, though not yet fully blossomed, was destined—according to her doting papa—to break more hearts in the very near future than she had gowns crammed in her closet. And if her auburn lustrous ringlets, flawless complexion and long-lashed hazel eyes were aught to go by, not to mention her sly coquettish smile, neither was he much mistaken.

The Falconers were not a wealthy family, though they managed tolerably well to give an impression of such to their rivals at large by maintaining a manor house in the country, their own carriage and four, and eight servants; furthermore they made sure to entertain all the right persons at respectable intervals, dress tastefully—if not in high fashion—and annually rent a house in the most sought after part of London for the Season, thus ensuring that they were seen with, and by, all the notables. True, their only son had not aspired to either Eton or Winchester, nevertheless, they had succeeded in keeping him at Oxford, whilst Sharonne (after shattering the nerves of her dear mamma and innumerable governesses) strove to master the intricate niceties, absolutely essential to a young lady of refinement, at a local, but highly estimable, seminary in their native Hertfordshire.

"Something amiss, m' boy?" questioned Sir Giles unexpectedly, catching his son unawares. "Appetite gone a-begging?"

Jonathan gulped down his apprehension. "I-I'm afraid I'm not very hungry, sir . . . I—er—did not sleep very well—"

"Oh, Jonathan, my dear boy, are you ill?" broke in his mother anxiously, wringing her hands across her non-existent bosom. "I must declare, you do look a little wan. Shall I ask cook to prepare—"

"I beg you will not fuss so, Mother," pleaded her despairing son. "I—I have a slight attack of the headache, that is all."

"Then a dose of my hartshorn, perhaps? Or some lime water?" she persisted, half rising from her chair.

"For heaven's sake, Agatha, sit down!" remonstrated Sir Giles with a grimace. "Dammit! Ye'll give us all the headache."

"Please don't distress yourself, Mother," Jonathan reassured her. "I shall be quite well anon."

"Huh!" declared Sharonne with defiant toss of glossy curls. "What can you expect, staggering up the stairs at two this morning?"

"Jonathan!" shrieked Lady Falconer, aghast. "Y-You weren't i-in . . . tox . . . ica . . . ted?"

A groan sounded from Sir Giles.

"N-No, Mother," replied Jonathan, scowling thunderously at his sister. "I was not intoxicated."

"Then why did you fall up the stairs and sleep in your clothes?" pursued Sharonne, undaunted.

"Because I was extremely tired, nothing more," exclaimed her brother, growing heated.

"But you said you didn't sleep very well?" parried she. "And what have you done to your eye?"

"Eye?" queried Sir Giles, dragging his attention from the choice ham on his fork.

"Eeek!" cried Lady Falconer upon catching sight of the offending optic. "Jonathan! What on earth is the matter with your eye?"

"I—I collided with a statue whilst walking in the park," submitted Jonathan, deeming it wiser to adhere to the excuse he had given the porter at White's.

Sister Sharonne gave licence to a peal of irritating laughter.

"Oh, Jonathan! Surely even you could concoct a more feasible lie?"

"Sharonne!" admonished her father.

"Sorry, Papa," submitted she meekly, with a flutter of her lashes.

"Aagh . . . I f-feel . . . f-faint," whimpered her mother, cherishing a forlorn hope she might do so before she heard the worst.

Sir Giles muttered a round unsympathetic curse. "Plague on't! Fetch y'r mother the hartshorn, damme, or burn some goose-feathers."

Sharonne hastened to oblige as her mother's wails waxed in pitch and volume, causing Jonathan to wonder how his dear mamma would take on when she anon discovered the full extent of his troubles.

"Confound it, Agatha, calm y'rself!" went on Sir Giles, loath to have his meal disrupted, especially by his

28

wife's interminable vapours. " 'Tis a simple enough mishap. Ofttimes done it m'self. Rot me, they will insist on setting the infernal things up in such ridiculous places."

"Your smelling-bottle, Mamma," ventured Sharonne, solicitously proffering the bottle.

"Aah-ah, th-thank you, child," gasped her ladyship, inhaling the fuming bottle as if it were the gateway betwixt life and death.

"And it was quite dark," Jonathan vindicated himself.

"Even so, dear brother," chuckled Sharonne impishly, "the statue seems to have taken monstrous exception."

"Oh, do hold your tongue, Sharonne," lamented her mother.

"Aye, minx," seconded Sir Giles, frowning disapprovingly at her. "Pay heed to y'r coddled egg and y'r manners. Hrumph! Too much licence over at Blaydon Beck—y'r Aunt Matilda allowin' ye to run amok wi' cloddish yokels, and gallop heaven knows where on unbroken colts,—"

"Lud! I might have guessed it," bewailed her ladyship, arms flung aloft in despair. "What other could possibly be held responsible but my sister! I do declare, if the very ceiling were to descend about our ears or the French invade our shores, it would be poor Matilda's blame."

"Gad, Agatha, no need to take on so!" exclaimed her spouse, as comfortingly as he knew how, wrestling to gain advantage over a mouthful of newly-baked bread. "Ye know I esteem y'r dear sister almost as highly as y'rself."

His wife's sharp eye stabbed him atop of the bottle, she certain that the remark was meant in a derogatory manner but unable to prove it.

"Anywise, puss, won't be long ere ye'll be gettin' packed off to finishin' school."

Sharonne's cutlery clattered on to her plate.

"F-Finishing school!" echoed she, horrified. "Oh, no, Father! Y-You don't mean it, you couldn't be so cruel!"

"There is no purpose in trying to cajole your father, Sharonne," stated Lady Falconer, rallying herself with superhuman effort to rebuke her offspring. "The matter has been discussed at great length and I—er—we have decided that a term or two at Mrs. Whittlebred's Academy for Young Ladies will not come amiss before your presentation next year."

"Hum, if y'r Aunt Matilda sees fit to supply the wherewithal as promised," pointed out Sir Giles, nurturing doubts.

"Indeed, husband," acknowledged his wife, finally relinquishing the precious bottle. "You now see why we cannot possibly afford to offend my dear sister?"

"But I can't be locked away for months!" screamed Sharonne, leaping afoot and flinging down her napkin. "It's uncivilised! I can't! I won't, never!"

"Oh dear," repined her ladyship, reaching instinctively for her life-giving bottle. "Now she's going to throw a tantrum."

"Sit down at once, girl, and cease behaving like a hoyden!" commanded Sir Giles, his irate visage turning from crimson to puce.

"Whatever are we to do with the child?" my lady wailed on, her eyes rolling deliriously round in her head

30

as the ammonia took powerful effect—while her son sat discreetly mumchance, thankful for this minor contention which was effectively diverting attention from himself, yet aware that his turn would come as inevitably as the Day of Judgment, and inwardly debated how he could break the news of his forthcoming duel without creating a full-scale family riot.

Sharonne remained standing rigidly by her chair, her head held high in an attitude of parental defiance, though emotional tension was evident in the way she twisted, unmercifully, the ribboned knots adorning the stomacher of her blue satin negligée.

"Sit down, I say!" bellowed Sir Giles, thumping the table with clenched fist. "Burn me, it's all been arranged! Y'r goin' to Mrs Whittlebed's Academy and that's an end on't!"

"Er—bred, Giles," corrected his wife, betwixt sniffs.

"Eh? Bread? Jonathan, offer y'r mother the bread. Egad! No need to issue a proclamation, Agatha—"

"No, dear," clarified her ladyship irritably. "It's Whittlebred, not 'bed."

"Ah! Haw—well, 'tis all one. She's goin' an' that's that!"

Appreciating that this was one of the rare occasions when her father was not to be inveigled from his decision, Sharonne plumped down in her chair to glower balefully at the half-devoured egg on her plate as if it were primarily responsible for her dire fate.

Silence descended, with nought to be heard but the occasional snort and belch from Sir Giles, sniffs from Sharonne as she fought back the tears pricking her eyes, and groans from her ladyship as she languished over her aromatic bottle—whilst Jonathan juggled the entire English language round in his brain in his efforts to phrase his staggering announcement as euphemistically as possible.

"F-Father," probed he when a courageous moment occurred. "H-Have you perchance heard tell of—of the —er—of the M-Marquess of—er—of A-Ashton?"

Sir Giles hesitated with cup poised two inches from his lips, eyeing his son curiously.

"Why should such a man be of any interest to you, boy?" he questioned brusquely.

Jonathan laughed nervously with a noncommittal gesture, trying to feign indifference.

"He is of no interest whatsoever, Father, I assure you. I—I simply chanced to hear his name r-rumoured."

His father seemed visibly relieved and replaced his cup upon its saucer.

"I am pleased to own that I am not on acquaintance with the scoundrel!" replied Sir Giles forcefully. "I merely know of him, which is sufficient for any man. Anyone of honour and decency would not be found associating with him. He a vile knave and a murderer and ought to be drummed out of society!"

Lady Falconer clicked her tongue in disfavour of her husband's indelicate tone.

"M-Murderer, Father?" stammered Jonathan.

"Humph, duellist if you prefer it, though I see nought to choose 'twixt 'em. Gad! He must have run through more vitals than I've downed bottles of claret, an' that's a fair few."

"If that is indeed so, Father," his pert daughter could not resist interpolating, "he must have killed off the entire population of London."

"I'll thank you to keep a civil tongue, chit," admonished Sir Giles, tweaking her nose.

"Jonathan!" exclaimed Lady Falconer again. "What ails you? You've gone as white as the tablecloth!"

Jonathan strove manfully to shake off the panic which suddenly gripped him.

"N-Nothing, Mother. I—I feel a little dizzy . . . probably because I haven't eaten—"

"I shall repair at once to the kitchen and have cook mix you a bowl of thin gruel," declared his mother adamantly, starting to her feet with surprising agility and quitting the room ere Jonathan could stop her, for the very thought of watery gruel made his stomach capsize.

"The M-Marquess is a skilled swordsman, F-Father?" he at length managed to falter.

"Aye, none has beaten him so far, though many would wish it otherwise."

"Why, brother dear?" gibed Sharonne, hitting much too near the mark. "Has he challenged you?"

Colour flooded back into Jonathan's cheeks as he rounded angrily on his sister.

"I'll thank you not to ask such stupid questions!" he blazed at her. "You're a silly child who should keep quiet and not thrust her nose in where it's not wanted!"

Tears welled again in Sharonne's beautiful eyes at this cruel outburst which seemed unjust in proportion to her transgression, and her lower lip trembled visibly.

This her father could not allow, but as he was about to intercede on her behalf, he was forestalled by his wife who returned at this point.

"Really, Jonathan! I can't imagine what has taken possession of you this morning. You ought not to address your sister in such harsh tone—you forget, she is but a child! Apologise to her at once! I'm sure she meant no harm."

Jonathan rose stiffly to attention, mumbled an apology, gave a jerky bow, and at sight of the bowl of steaming nauseating gruel clasped in his mother's hands, hastened from the room.

3

IF BROTHER JONATHAN were harbouring a secret, Sharonne considered it no more than her sisterly duty to discover what it was, and so, with her over-developed sense of curiosity fully alerted it did not take her very long to run her brother to earth in one of the dingy garrets at the top of the house, where he had sought to take refuge away from further family interrogation, and humiliation.

The garret had, until quite recently, been occupied by a parlour-maid who had been discovered liberally sampling Sir Giles's best smuggled brandy and had consequently been dismissed on the spot with a sound whipping.

But Jonathan's haven was no longer a secret unto himself, and though he may lay claim to a tolerable success in deceiving his parents at the breakfast table, his inquisitive young sister, it would seem, was not so easily hoodwinked.

Sharonne tip-toed stealthily up the last flight of stairs, holding her breath and grimacing in annoyance when the second step from the top emitted a low groan beneath her weight, before she tip-toed on to halt outside the door of the garret embracing her brother. Stooping almost double, she peered with one eye through the keyhole to have her suspicions amply confirmed at sight of him drooping in an old broken Windsor chair, with a candle guttering on a three-legged stool in front of him. His head, with its carroty hair tied roughly back in a thin black ribbon, was clasped in his hands, woebegone fashion, and at intervals he brushed one huge cuff of his brown frock-coat across his eyes and gave a loud sniff.

Sharonne took a swift step backwards, clapping a hand over her mouth to stifle a gasp of alarm. Her brother was crying! He was actually crying, something she had never seen him do since he was nine years old when his favourite pony had injured a leg and had had to be shot. Misgiving seized her heart, for what had appealed to her as a girlish prank belowstairs now filled her with foreboding.

Gulping down her qualms, she at length scratched upon the door, which she knew was sure to be locked.

"J-Jonathan?" she whimpered plaintively through the keyhole. "L-Let me in, please."

The chair gave a loud creak and the sniffing stopped abruptly, followed by a short, poignant silence.

"G-Go away, Sh-Sharonne," came her brother's unsteady voice anon.

"But I want to help, truly."

"You c-can't . . . n-no one can. . . ."

"Oh, Jonathan, please! I promise not to tease, nor tell anyone."

"No, Sharonne!"

"Very well then, I shall go and fetch Papa!" declared she pettishly, straightening up to stomp off.

A louder creak from the chair followed by the hasty thud of feet on bare boards, and the door flew wide to admit the curious Sharonne—as she suspected it might—then it was immediately locked again.

"Well?" she breathed anxiously, once she was securely inside.

"Well what?" snapped Jonathan sullenly, storming back to the chair under the small high-set window. "It doesn't say because I've let you in that I'm going to tell you all my affairs. I did it to avoid rousing the entire household with your accursed tantrums!"

His sister looked commensurately crestfallen. "But you must tell someone, Jonathan, if something's troubling you very badly, or you'll make yourself sick. And I'm the only one you've got to tell."

"You're too young, Shar. You're only a child."

"I'm not a child! I'm sixteen!" she retorted indignantly, stamping her beslippered foot. "Many girls are married at my age."

"That's another thing—you're a girl, to boot. Even if you could help y-you'd never . . . under . . . stand. . . ." His voice trailed mournfully away and his head again sank between his hands. "I—I've no right . . . to b-burden y-you . . . with m-my . . . troubles . . ."

"Jonathan," cried Sharonne, increasingly alarmed to see him so dejected as she hastened to his side to place a comforting dimpled arm about his shoulders. "You must tell me! What is it? What have you done?"

"S-Some . . . thing . . . t-terrible," he moaned into his palms.

"What? What? Tell me for goodness sake! Or better still, why not tell Papa?"

"No! I can't . . . i-it's an affair of honour."

Sharonne gaped in wide-eyed horror. "Y-You mean that I was right after all? Oh, no, Jonathan, y-you aren't going to actually f-fight a d-duel?"

Jonathan nodded in abject despair.

"With this man called Ashton?"

He nodded again.

"Oh, Jonathan!" she lamented, stricken, collapsing with a rustle of silks upon the servant's palliasse behind the door. "You've never fought a duel in your life! Whatever will Mamma and Papa say?"

"Nothing! Because they aren't going to find out. You must promise on oath, Sharonne, not to breathe a word of this."

"But how on earth did it come about? What did you do to provoke the man?"

Jonathan sat up erect to stare fixedly at the cracked wall opposite.

"It happened last night, a-at White's. I overheard him making mock of Henrietta—sullying her unblemished reputation with his vile tongue. And so, I leapt up and challenged him—as any upright, honest gentleman would do!"

"Wouldn't he apologise?" she queried, guilelessly.

"Apologise!" ejaculated her brother with scathing contempt. "His sort wouldn't apologise if his carriage and six trampled down his own grandam!" He paused, throwing her a sheepish look. "Er—there was also an incident with w-wine," he confessed ruefully.

"Wine?"

"I-In his face."

"Oh, no!" groaned Sharonne, wondering if this were the limit of her brother's tribulations. "What possessed you to do such a dreadful thing? Were you so *very* drunk?"

"I-I'd seen it done before s-somewhere," stammered he, evading her last question, "—quite effectively. B-But s-somehow it . . . didn't . . . succeed."

The knuckles of Jonathan's perspiring hands glowed white as he wrung them in desperation, his eyes travelling to Sharonne's sweet dimpled face to linger in frantic appeal, hoping against all odds that she, with her lively ingenuity, might be able to suggest something which would rescue him from the gaping jaws of the terrible fate.

Sharonne stared back at him, scarce daring to credit her brother's look of mute entreaty, what he was demanding of her in that look, her—his junior by three years and a mere female, as he had informed her a few moments since in such derogatory manner. But despite all, she loved him dearly and felt a warm surge of pride in her ripening bosom that he was turning to her in this, his hour of greatest need, which played havoc with her latent maternal instinct, for he had never begged anything of her before, certainly nothing of such vital consequence as his very life! And so she donned her air of importance, as her mamma was wont to do, straightened her frilled linen cap, and fixed him with a determined eye.

"Very well, Jonathan," she announced adroitly. "We must waste no more time repining in self-pity. We must decide what's to be done to resolve the situation without delay. How long do we have?"

Jonathan consulted his silver-mounted watch with an air of defeat.

"Almost two hours."

"Two hours!" cried Sharonne, aghast.

"—before his second calls and blows the whole thing to Father."

"Then he must be stopped."

"How?" queried her brother with derisive laugh, already visualising himself laid to rest in the family vault. "Waylay and kidnap him?"

"Don't be absurd, Jonathan," she rebuked his childish satire with scorn. "I shall simply pay a personal call upon this Lord Ashton and—"

"Y-You'll *what*?" spluttered he, doubting if he had heard aright.

"—and intercede on your behalf," she completed unperturbed, as if she were making out a shopping inventory. "I shall act for you as your—what is the term, second?—and try to reason with him, persuade him to accept an apology on the grounds of over-fatigue, over-intoxication, or failing all else—insanity."

A strangulated gasp erupted from her brother.

"I-Insanity!" he exploded, red in the face. "Gad! You're the one who's bound for Bedlam!"

Sharonne tut-tutted in disapproval—another mannerism she had acquired from her mamma. "For goodness sake, Jonathan, do calm yourself," she besought him in dulcet tone. "I vow 'tis nothing personal. What doth it matter if he believes you truly mad, and even has you committed, if it will save your life? Following your outlandish conduct last night he is probably convinced you are, anyway."

"Insane or not, Shar, I can't go hat in hand begging his forgiveness! It just isn't done! It's flatly against the code!"

"I never suggested for one moment that you should!" retaliated she, growing every bit as exasperated as he. "I shall apologise on your behalf. I don't mind humbling myself. I-It's somehow easier for a female—"

"No, Sharonne, it's too dangerous by half! I've told you already, you're only a child!"

Sharonne bristled at his continued allusion to her immaturity.

"What you don't seem to realise, Jonathan Falconer, is that your life is at stake!" she shouted at him, fighting back the grief choking her. "And whether you approve or not, I am determined to do all in my power to save it, even if it means grovelling at the feet of this—this —insufferable man to the point of sacrificing my honour—"

Jonathan unleashed a savage oath. "Don't be a fool, Sharonne! You don't understand a word you're saying!"

This was largely true, though his sister did not particularly care to be informed of the fact. As she still had her honour to sacrifice, she saw no harm in proclaiming the information at every opportunity to further her advantage. Besides which, it sounded very impressive and every lady of quality cried it aloud when they wished to create a dramatic effect.

"However, I'm certain it won't amount to that," she breezed on, impervious to his outburst. "Most gentlemen of breeding are extremely courteous to young ladies of refinement, and I can be most persuasive when the fancy takes me, Jonathan, as you very well know," declared she, adding emphasis to her claim with an unashamed ogle in his direction, which did nought to transform his original opinion, but, on the contrary, convinced him that his dear naïve sister would never again see the light of day should she happen to ogle the Marquess of Ashton in like manner. "Furthermore," appended she, with vainglorious toss of her golden curls, "I shall take Letty with me for protection."

"Letty couldn't protect a cockroach!" he rebuffed her, leaping up to stride about the dismal garret like a caged lion awaiting its dinner, his fingers running through his red hair—for whilst he was ready to admit to the element of truth in his sister's words he was certainly not prepared to sacrifice her precious innocence to save his own worthless skin. "I forbid you to go, Sharonne! You're a silly schoolroom chit who doesn't know what she's about. One would think it were the vicar you were going to visit, instead of the most notorious rake in London. This Lord Ashton has not earned his infamous repute by merely tumbling dairymaids in a haystack, or flinging stones at the barber's cat!"

"Well? Can you think of a better idea?" she countered tartly, as the sadly diminished candle finally spluttered out, leaving the two cloaked in sympathetic shadows.

Jonathan ceased his pacing to shrug his youthful shoulders disconsolately, unable to proffer any alternative suggestion.

"Then there is no more to be said on the matter, Jonathan," she resumed, struggling to her feet from the palliasse and shaking out her gown with an air of finality, for it was the very first time she had defeated brother Jonathan in argument and intended to savour the moment as long as possible. "If I leave at once I shall at least be able to prevent his second calling upon Papa, even if I achieve nought else. Do you have his direction?"

Jonathan flung away from her with a stifled sob as if the whole business were too execrable to even contemplate, let alone act upon.

"Jonathan," overtured his sister compassionately, approaching him gently from behind. "Please don't distress yourself any further, for I feel sure all will be well. I may be young and a stupid girl, but I'm also your sister who loves you very dearly. I must do this to help you—I must! I feel it is the only answer, and I promise to take extreme care, I swear. If you prefer it, I shall take James with me for extra protection, but I'm loath to attract too much attention lest Mamma or Papa discovers all."

Still her brother did not respond, but after a moment's further hesitation he fumbled in his pocket and ultimately withdrew the Marquess's card which he pushed into her hand in dumb surrender.

"Thank you, Jonathan," she breathed, planting an eager kiss upon his cheek. "You do understand how vital it is that one of us goes to see this Lord Ashton, don't you? And as you obviously cannot, then I must."

4

IT WAS upon pretext of a sudden urgent need to purchase a set of matching ribbons to embellish her newest gown that Sharonne effected an escape from beneath her mamma's vigilant eye that morning, for no servant could surely be trusted upon such a vital errand.

Before Lady Falconer could query the urgency of her daughter's mission, Sharonne, in company with her maid Letty, had quitted the house and was already two blocks away *en route* to Berkeley Square where was situated the imposing mansion of my Lord Marquess. Letty had no reason to disbelieve her mistress's concocted excuse until they passed by the haberdasher's shop without venturing within its portals, when Sharonne informed her maid that she really nurtured the intention of visiting a certain lady friend of whom her mother firmly disapproved—generating the doubt in Letty's head whether the friend were indeed of the feminine gender.

It was not difficult at this stage for Sharonne to feel confident, so confident in fact that the possibility of failing in her quest never once crossed her mind, for was not Jonathan wont to boast about the daring young bucks in his fashionable circle, and therefore likely to exaggerate their wicked repute and prowess with the sword and ladies in order to impress? But at first awe-inspiring sight of Ashton House she did not feel nearly so brave, though she gave not the slightest intimation of this to Letty who sidled instinctively behind her mistress's voluminous hoop-petticoats as they approached the austere mahogany door, which was elaborately carved with feathered scrolls, dominated over by an eagle in flight, and gleamed in evidence of fastidious care.

Swallowing hard, Sharonne bade Letty wait outside, assuring her that she would not be above ten minutes, before she ventured up the stone steps to the forbidding door with its shining brass knocker fashioned as an eagle's head—an uncommon close relation of the one above. Grasping the knocker firmly, she gave two loud bangs at the offending door as if defying herself to uplift her petticoats and take her heels, which she felt a sudden overwhelming impulse to do, and indeed would have done but for the thought of what Jonathan's fate would otherwise be.

Scarcely had she released the knocker when the door swung ajar to reveal an arrogant flunkey in powdered wig and the Ashton livery of purple and gold who, curt of bow, enquired her business in a tone quite as frigid as his disposition. His attitude served in some measure, however, to quell Sharonne's apprehension and goad her to reply quite as superciliously as he that she wished to see his master the Marquess upon a matter of extreme urgency. Following a further, more thorough, inspection the lackey deigned to invite her into the spacious hall where he suggested she seat herself whilst he betook himself up the thick-carpeted stairs to the salon on the first floor.

As the only chairs available were of uncushioned solid oak, and not at all suited to receiving a bell hoop with the respect it deserved, she remained standing, nervously tweaking errant curls into place beneath her beflowered chip-hat whilst critically viewing herself in a ponderous gilt-framed mirror at hand, and wondering what manner of man was this Lord Ashton and how readily he would succumb to her coquettish wiles.

She was absorbed in the flow of her gown's modest train when the footman returned to inform her, more frigidly than before, that his master was otherwise engaged and expected to be for some considerable while. Perhaps the young mistress could call again at some more convenient hour?

It was useless to protest. The menial's very attitude told her that this would avail her nought but the humiliating alternative of a forcible ejection, from which he would no doubt derive more than a modicum of satisfaction. On the other hand, Miss Falconer was extremely reluctant to take her leave and admit defeat so early in the proceedings. It was lacking but one hour to noon, which allowed her no time to call back again. Consequently, she was obliged to rely upon a little subterfuge, appreciating that once outside of the door her chances of getting on the inside again would prove remote indeed.

"Good sir," she fluttered her long lashes at the frosty-visaged footman as provocatively as she knew how. "I should be loath to come again at another inopportune moment, and as my business with his lordship is a matter of life and death, perhaps you would be kind enough to enquire of your master the precise hour he would have me call?"

The lackey was thrown out of countenance and deviated—but momentarily—loath to interrupt his master a second time, yet equally loath to refuse what was a perfectly reasonable request, while Sharonne sought to influence his decision in her favour with a disarming smile, certain that 'neath the stony exterior there must surely lurk a human being. Neither, seemingly, was she mistaken, for the lackey suddenly gave a jerky bow and departed a second time for the august presence of his master.

Barely was he out of sight when Sharonne took her chance and, opening the great door, she banged it shut again as thunderously as she could, then took swift refuge beneath the stairs, waiting with bated breath for the footman's dumbfounded return, and for him to take himself off upon the assumption that she had departed. All went according to plan, and when his feet had died away to his quarters she crept out from her hiding place and up the stairs without a sound. Upon reaching the first floor, she was confronted with a choice of no less than five doors and stood awhile nonplussed, wondering which to begin with, appreciating that time was becoming her worst enemy—when a gentleman's infectious laughter issued from behind door number four. The laughter would seem to augur well, that she had found my Lord Marquess in cheerful spirits.

Certain that this must be the gentleman she sought, she took a deep breath, gritted her strong white teeth, and burst into the room.

Sharonne found herself immediately thrown at a disadvantage by a blaze of sunshine from the huge windows, glinting upon white marble and gold which seemed to be everywhere, and momentarily blinded her; gold velvet upholstered chairs and settees, curtains of gold thread, gilded furniture, flashing crystal, and pillars of white Italian marble, while gold brocade hangings and Venetian mirrors shimmered upon the walls.

As her vision grew accustomed to the brilliance and splendour of her surroundings it eventually alighted upon the occupants, namely, two gentlemen reclining in chairs upon either side of the ornate fireplace of sculptured blue-veined marble. The two were conversing in subdued tone, obviously something of a confidential nature until it was rudely disrupted by Miss Falconer's entrance.

My Lord Ravenby's false eyebrows swept aloft in astonishment before he mounted to his feet and gave a hesitant bow, his neatly bewigged head pivoting betwixt his companion and the newcomer as if seeking to establish a common factor, while the Marquess of Ashton still languished unconcernedly in his chair, indolently swinging a pomander to and fro as if the unwarranted intrusion of attractive young females were an everyday occurrence in his household.

Lord Ashton was clad in a banyan of pink-and-white gossamer silk which stressed the deception of his childlike innocence; his long fair hair, brushed till it gleamed like silver in the morning sunshine, and resting in soft waves upon his shoulders. As he was the only one in undress, Sharonne rightly assumed him to be the gentleman she sought.

Oddly enough, she was more taken aback than anyone, for the Marquess was not at all what she had expected. But then, what exactly had she expected? Certainly not one quite so . . . so . . . what was the word—saint-like? Surely Jonathan was mistaken? How could one so delicate, so pale and fragile, possibly harm anyone? On the contrary, she found herself fighting an irresistible urge to mother him, cherish and protect him, so vulnerable did he seem.

In a voice as lethargic as his demeanour, he eventually broke the pregnant silence.

"A friend of yours, Rave?"

"N-No, Gabe," stammered Lord Ravenby, lowering himself gradually back into the chair as his host was making no effort to rise and do the honours. "Forsooth! I was about to ask you the same question."

The Marquess flung the new arrival a glance of phlegmatic disdain.

"Well, Miss—er—?"

"F-Falconer," she supplied hurriedly, venturing cautiously nearer, her wide hazel eyes riveted upon his inanimate figure. "Miss Sh-Sharonne Falconer, a-an it please you."

"It pleaseth me not one whit, Miss Falconer," he responded with cold indifference. "And I'd thank you to close the door—"

"Certainly, sir—er—your l-lordship!" gushed Sharonne, eagerly making to oblige.

"—on your way out."

Sharonne closed the door but admantly stood her ground upon the inside, though her heart and brain pounded in advanced stages of perturbation, for now that she was actually in the lion's lair the situation somehow seemed rather different to blithely discussing it at home in the garret with her brother. But she was here in Ashton House, and she had a purpose to fulfil, so rallying all her resources to Jonathan's cause she turned to confront the Marquess.

"I—I come to crave a boon of you, my Lord Marquess," she declared, the epitome of defiance with her back adhered to the door. "And I refuse to leave until it is granted—or at least heard."

The Marquess hesitated, pomander suspended, viewing through narrowed eyes this audacious creature who presumed to make demands of him.

"Refuse?" he queried on a suspicious note. "An ill-chosen word for one in your precarious position. A somewhat indiscreet beginning, Miss Falconer. One does not burst uninvited into the devil's domain then cheerfully issue ultimatums."

Sharonne bit her lip at her folly and casting caution aside swept up to his chair and sank into a profound curtsy of contrition in a diversion of strategy.

"P-Please forgive me, my lord," she begged brokenly, embedding her strong teeth in her lower lip to draw tears of anguish to her soulful gaze, designed to dissolve his lordship's icy shell and reduce him to a quivering mass of gentlemanly solicitude. " 'Tis my extreme anxiety which compels me to make so boldly with my tongue. I—I come upon a matter of the utmost urgency! Something which only your lordship can rectify and ease my terrible burden—"

"Ecod, Gabe!" ejaculated Lord Ravenby. "Not another! 'Pon rep, that must make a round dozen this month!"

Silence prevailed as the Marquess casually elevated a lightly pencilled eyebrow to survey Sharonne in greater detail, from top to toe.

"Faith, can't say I recollect the face . . . nor the figure . . ." he drawled, his attention drifting back to the pomander which was apparently of more interest, "but I s'pose that is of little significance."

" 'S blood, man!" vituperated his friend. "You must have populated half the country!"

All this observation evoked from his friend was a

yawn of resignation to the inevitable outcome of his reckless pleasures.

"Well? What is your price? 'S life, being of blood-stock you'll want the brat in comfort, I presume?"

Sharonne turned a variety of colours as she emitted a gasp of outrage, her suspicions amply confirmed that he actually mistook her for one of his conquests.

"Gadzooks!" erupted my Lord Ravenby in a sudden flash of inspiration, before flames had a chance to belch from the lady's quivering nostrils. "Stap me if Falconer an't the name of the young varlet we encountered last eve, Gabe," he hissed as tactfully as he could manage in the other's ear in order to avoid further embarrassment. "The youth I'm due to call upon at noon this very day!"

It was here that Sharonne's indignation excelled the bounds of decorum and she leapt up from her host's elegant feet, seething at the affront.

"H-How dare you, sir! How dare you insinuate such a vile wicked thing! To think that I would descend to the despicable depths of allowing you to—to—"

"Yes?" he parried calmly.

To her further mortification she found it a sheer impossibility to put what she had in mind into ladylike King's English and so could do little but stand over his supine form, fuming like an alchemist's laboratory.

"Surely the idea is not so inconceivable with your endowment of charms? Hm, a trifle immature, perhaps," he mused, permitting his seductive gaze to wander at will over her ripening form, "but your luck might turn in a year or two—who can tell? Aye, I could well be tempted. . . ."

Sharonne stood before him livid with rage, for no

one had presumed to speak so to her before. Valiantly, she fought to endure the insult and keep sharp rein on her tongue, for to attack him at this crucial stage would be to relinquish all hope for Jonathan. Moreover, perhaps she really ought to be thankful that the Marquess did consider her too immature, for if he had elected to, well, do whatever men like he did to females, there and then upon the sumptuous fur rug before the fireplace, there would have been decidedly little she could have done to prevent him. Besides, had not that been her original motive in coming to Berkeley Square—to barter herself for Jonathan's life?

Suddenly she no longer trembled in anger, but in panic, as Lord Ashton rose slowly to his feet, his hard ruthless eyes not once deviating from her face. She stood tensed, rooted to the floor, bethinking he had suffered a change of heart, and so expected any moment to be seized and ravished on the spot, with Lord Ravenby a reluctant, though totally ineffectual, bystander.

But nought was farther from her host's mind, who, to her speechless amazement, swept her a graceful leg whilst enquiring the reason for her unexpected advent and how he could be of service. And although his lips curled in the ghost of a smile, his pale blue eyes remained cold and inexorable.

One need hardly say that Sharonne lost no time in taking full advantage of this wholly unexpected offer and so embarked upon the longest and most heart-rending supplication guaranteed to wrought emotional devastation within the human breast. She begged and pleaded as only a female of the species knoweth how, coaxed and cajoled, threatened and provoked! Bribed

52

him! Tempted and beguiled him! And finally implored him upon bended knee to spare her dear brother who was nought but a silly impetuous boy!

Perhaps it was to the Marquess's credit that he heard her supplication without interruption, futhermore, seemed to digest her words, urging Sharonne to give the most outstanding performance of her life and which would have assuredly reduced her father, Sir Giles, to tears even in his most obdurate mood. But she was not pleading with her father. Neither was the breast, whose emotions was endeavouring to devastate, of the human variety.

The silence which greeted her final imprecation seemed never-ending, during which she stood breathlessly before the ruler of her brother's fate, waiting, hoping that when he did condescend to answer it would be what she wished to hear.

"Do you come here in the capacity of your brother's second? Or as his peace-offering?" he enquired eventually.

"I come not as a peace-offering, my lord, but as peace-maker," she countered swiftly. "I see no reason why blood should be shed when a simple apology would set all to rights. My brother is quite willing to apologise. All you have to do is accept his apology with good grace. Surely that isn't too much to ask? Granted, it may mean losing face on his part, but as I explained to him only this morning, 'tis better than losing his life! I-Is it n-not, my l-lord?"

Her voice trailed timidly away to turbulent breathing, for the Marquess now loomed over her, so close that the delicate aroma of the unguents with which he nourished his tender skin pervaded her senses as she still waited patiently for him to grant a yea or nay to her plea. Indeed, the fact that he withheld his comments for such an inordinate length of time would seem to augur well for Jonathan, she was thinking, when Lord Ashton gave licence to a burst of the most diabolical laughter Sharonne had ever heard, which sent shivers shooting down her spine. On the contrary, this would not seem to augur well!

"Let it not be said, Miss Falconer, that the Marquess of Ashton denied you fair hearing," he observed, amiably enough. "Er—you have done craving your boon, I presume?

Sharonne nodded, apprehensively.

"Very well, you shall now have my answer," he went on in the same vein—though his eyes remained hard as flint. "Kindly return from whence you came and inform your silly impetuous brother that I expect him to be at the Ring in Hyde Park, two days hence—"

"No! No! My lord, I beg you—" she cried in alarm, wondering how he could have misinterpreted her plea so adversely.

"—at crack of dawn," he completed nonchalantly, as if he were passing remarks upon the weather instead of someone's death sentence.

"Should he fail to appear, I shall take it upon myself to call in person at number nine, Albemarle Street, and drag him out by—"

"Oh, no! Y-You couldn't! My m-mother! F-Father! The scandal!" she protested wildly, wringing her hands over her heaving bosom.

"Then I suggest you take the appropriate measures to ensure that he keeps the appointment."

54

"B-But he's only a b-boy, my lord . . . h-he's only nineteen!"

"Whether he be nineteen or ninety, if he chooseth to live like a man he must be equally prepared to die like one."

"Y-You don't understand. He laboured under strain —tiredness—a broken heart—"

"If he laboured 'neath anything, mistress, I should say 'twas acute intoxication which, even so, does not vindicate his outlandish conduct."

"Lord Ashton, were not you once his age? Did not you ever act impetuously thus?" Sharonne furthered her entreaty, tears now springing readily to her eyes without the need to resort to devious arts.

"Yes!" he snapped caustically. "And suffered the consequences."

My Lord Ravenby, who had secreted himself discreetly betwixt a firescreen and a tall pedestal stand, hoping thereby that his presence might be overlooked, now found conscience and duty goading him into support of his friend.

"If you will forgive the intrusion, ma'am," he ventured with a respectful cough as he bowed out from his niche.

"Allow me to say on his lordship's behalf that there have been encounters too numerous to mention whereby Lord Ashton has proved the aggressor—in truth, I feel certain he himself would be first to corroborate this. . . ." He paused, rotating a wary eye in the vicinity of his companion in the forlorn hope of his verbal support, but the Marquess was too absorbed in the dangle of his pomander, and so Lord Ravenby continued, unabashed. "Duty governs my tongue, ma'am, I must speak out. Upon this occasion Lord Ashton is beyond reproach! Your brother did offer the most intense provocation to his lordship. He was given no choice but to accept your brother's challenge." Another bow, and Lord Ravenby seated himself unobtrusively in the corner, as the Marquess resumed command.

"Your brother is abundantly aware that the duel is not of my choosing. 'S life, very few are, though none would believe it so. Alas, the price one must pay for being a reputed swordhand is the curse of being plagued to an untimely grave by young bloods out to prove their mettle."

Sharonne swallowed hard and took a hesitant step forward.

"I-I'm sure he didn't mean to be offensive, Lord Ashton—"

"Permit me to correct you, dear child," he observed blandly. "He wasn't offensive."

"H-He wasn't?"

"Nay, he was damned hostile! I swear 'twas open warfare from the outset! And if 'tis warfare he wants, then 'tis warfare he will get, two days hence at swordpoint. Good den to you, Mistress Falconer."

She was being dismissed! No, this she could not allow without one final desperate attempt to sway him from his bloodthirsty objective.

"L-Lord Ashton, y-you can't mean to g-go through with it!" she sobbed frantically, dogging his beslipped heels round the expansive room. "I-It would be cold-blooded murder!"

"You forget," he reminded her in blasé fashion, regaling his delicately arched nostrils with the pomander's rare perfume, "he has two days in which to improve his technique."

"Two days! It would take a lifetime to——"

"Ah, now there I can be of service, mistress," he apprised her with marked condescension. "I recommend him to Monsieur Fougére, fencing master *extraordinaire,* of Covent Garden. He has my permission to mention me by name——"

"He's my brother! He's too young to die!" she screamed, wildly distraught, finally relinquishing all hope as she began to appreciate the true extent of this man's demoniacal cruelty, for he seemed to be actually enjoying the drama, to be revelling in her misfortune, as if it appeased some dire craving essential to his existence, like food and drink. And the duel itself——was he also anticipating with the same nauseating relish the carving up of her brother's sweet innocent flesh?

Demented with anguish and hatred of the vile heartless being before her, who prized a scented bauble higher than human life, Sharonne lost her reason and snatching the offending pomander out of the Marquess's long white fingers, flung it furiously across the room to shatter a large Baroque mirror opposite, which fell in a dozen jagged pieces upon the Persian carpet. True she had not intended to break such a valuable piece, nor, indeed, anything at all, but this was a matter of sheer indifference to my Lord Marquess who rounded on her, his comely face distorted with a look of intense rage——no ordinary rage, but one of underlying evil, as if seized with a fiendish intent to do . . . what?

To term Sharonne terrified rigid would be no overstatement. As she had never had cause to experience the dire feeling hitherto, she was somewhat at a loss to know how to react to the unprecedented situation, for her dear father had never eyed her in such a way, nor Jonathan, and they were virtually the only men she had ever known. Therefore, she could do little but to retreat from my lord, trembling step by trembling step, until she felt the bow-fronted mahogany cabinet at her back. So petrified with fear, it was some time ere she could make coherent sound, as the Marquess continued to slowly, menacingly, advance.

"I-I'm s-sorry . . . b-believe me, I—I . . . r-really d-didn't . . . m-mean—" She broke off with a tiny squeak, for the Marquess was now close—uncomfortably close!

She swiftly lowered her gaze to the gaily patterned carpet, loath to witness the satanic look in those implacable eyes. But he determined that she should, and brutally jerked up her face to his.

"You begin to annoy me, Miss Falconer," he snarled, his voice choked with venom. "I suggest you take your leave whilst you are yet at liberty to do so. Consider yourself fortunate that you are still of too tender an age to appeal to my sensitive taste."

"I-I'll g-go at once, m-my l-lord," gasped she, ready to fade away with relief that she was to be spared the variety of gruesome retributions currently flashing through her mind. "P-Please, j-just grant me your a-assurance that your s-second w-will not c-call at my home, and I-I'll be g-gone."

The Marquess pushed her roughly aside and turned away.

"You have my word—now get out!"

But ere his voice died away, Sharonne was already gone!

5

CONTRARY to external impressions, Sharonne's call upon the Marquess of Ashton had not proved entirely futile. Indeed, she had learnt a great deal during the brief though turbulent interlude with him, which served to hasten her metamorphosis from the naïve immature girl into the spirited young woman she was destined to become.

Try how she may, she simply could not summon the heart to break the sad truth to her brother and diverted her return to Albemarle Street through Green Park to gain the time she needed to seek a solution to the problem. With Letty mutely by her side, she sat for a considerable while gazing pensively at the fashionable ladies and their sycophantic admirers sauntering by, as she searched frantically in her mind for any possible means whereby Jonathan might acquit himself honourably of the dire fate looming over his dear head—but, alas, no such idea occurred.

Nevertheless, one idea certainly did occur, so perilous that Sharonne would never have given it credence only a matter of minutes ago, but now everything was different, not least of all herself. She was not the same Sharonne Falconer who had ventured gullibly into Ashton House that very morn, but someone of wider vision, experience of life, and what lay beneath the courteous facade of gentlemanly etiquette. Even so, she was at first extremely reluctant to adopt this plan, but ultimately was compelled to acknowledge it the only way in which she could guarantee to save the brother she loved. And so, she rose resolutely to her feet, smoothing the folds from her rumpled gown, determined that Providence decreed it her duty to take this precarious step on Jonathan's behalf.

Thus decided, Sharonne returned home, and striving her level best to affect a light-hearted mien broke the wonderful news to the anxious Jonathan that all was forgiven, that the Most Honourable Marquess of Ashton had deigned to accept his abject apology. So overwhelming was his relief and gratitude that for several seconds her brother did not know quite what to say and instead hugged and kissed his sister, then promptly broke down and wept like a child, vowing from the depths of his heart that he would never get himself into such a predicament again as long as he lived.

When granted an opportune moment Sharonne adjourned to her room to devote meticulous thought to her scheme and establish her *modus operandi*. Once this was fully detailed in her mind she concentrated upon conducting herself in as normal a manner as possible in order that no one—least of all Jonathan—should suspect what she was about.

However, she was not able to put the first stage of her plan into motion until the following evening when Jonathan was engaged in a game of chess with their father in the parlour, leaving his room vacant long enough for his sister to venture therein and appropriate a suit of cinnamon superfine, a camlet cloak, and all the essential trappings to a young gentleman of the day, including the largest hat she could find. She paused, wistfully eyeing her most vital piece of equipment, his full-length Toledo rapier, but resisted the impulse to take it as yet, for she knew Jonathan was accustomed to sleeping within reach of its comforting protection—a habit he had acquired at Oxford—and would therefore be sure to remark its absence.

Consequently, it was not until half an hour before dawn on the fateful morning of the duel, that Sharonne crept stealthily into her brother's room and took the weapon whilst he lay rapt in blissful dreams, far removed from cold reality. Aware that it could well be the last time she would ever gaze upon him, Sharonne longed to bestow a farewell kiss upon his fair cheek, but managed to resist the impulse lest she waken him.

And so, clad in Jonathan's clothes, with the large-brimmed hat concealing her long golden tresses and overshadowing her face, she crept off down the stairs, the rapier clutched avidly in one clammy hand and buckled shoes in the other. Upon reaching the parlour she was suddenly gripped in the throes of panic and to prevent herself galloping headlong back to the comforting haven of her room she availed herself of her father's brandy which prompted prodigious coughing which she trusted would not waken the servants prematurely.

Upon regaining her composure she continued on through the parlour, along the passage to the kitchen, scullery, to the rear entrance where, scarce daring to breathe, she withdrew the bolts, lifted the latch and slipped out into the engulfing darkness. At the corner where Albemarle Street converged with Piccadilly she paused to don shoes and sword by the flickering light of a flambeau, then glanced furtively all around before setting off to the right in the direction of Hyde Park, her step and bravura invigorated by the brandy which blazed in her veins.

As her footsteps rang out on the cobbles the first grey light of dawn appeared, and though there was little chance of meeting anyone able to recognise her Sharonne, nevertheless, deemed it circumspect to divert her route from the main road along Halfmoon Street to Curzon Street and on down past Chesterfield House to Tyburn Lane where the rural parkland of Hyde lay outstretched before her in the cold light of the new day, but even so, little could be distinguished in the ghostly morning mist which still blanketed the air.

She hastened across to the park, straining eyes and ears for evidence of anyone, but all remained unnaturally quiet, save for the distant sound of the first arrivals to the great city, bringing their wares from the surrounding villages and countryside to sell in the markets and streets. Here she quickened her pace even more, for dawn had broken and she had yet to find the Ring —a simple enough task upon a clear day, but in the swirling mist everything looked irritatingly the same.

Sharonne pressed on, to suddenly pull up short with a gasp upon discerning not far ahead the outline of four figures, and to hear the snorts and jingling harnesses of their accompanying steeds. She stood awhile in order to steady her palpitating heartbeat with three deep breaths, then ventured bravely forward to find the four consisting of my Lord Marquess, fashionably arrayed in mulberry superfine embellished with gold braid, and sporting a feathered plume in his jaunty cocked hat; his personal man, who was hanging upon my lord's elegant heels; his second, Lord Ravenby, just as fashionably, though less flamboyantly clad in brown stuff coat with gold trimmings; and finally, a surgeon of supposedly unbiased opinion.

" 'Pon my soul, Rave, I do believe the upstart cometh after all," exclaimed the Marquess, evidently in good spirits as he drew the group's attention to Sharonne stumbling through a patch of undergrowth, the rapier falling foul on her left foot. "Good den t' ye, stripling! 'Fore gad, we were about to despair o' ye and cry craven. Were we not, gentlemen?"

"I—I give you good day, gentlemen," responded Sharonne with a bow, lowering her voice an octave to masculine level.

Having dispensed the greetings, Lord Ravenby assumed command of the proceedings, indicating the area of marked ground which he invited Sharonne to peruse at her pleasure as she apparently had no second to undertake the duty for her, which my lord saw fit to point out somewhat superfluously.

"Er—you have no second, young sir."

"N-No, my lord. D-Does that mean the d-duel cannot t-take p-place?" questioned she, hopefully.

"Not exactly. It is a trifle unconventional but entirely within the code if both sides are agreeable, and you yourself are willing to accept the consequences."

"I see," replied she, crestfallen, head lowered the while to evade his eye, as with a click of heels Lord Ravenby turned away.

Meanwhile, my Lord Marquess was losing no time as he permitted his valet to relieve him of his coat, hat and claret-and-gold waistcoat, in preparation for the fray—at sight of which something akin to fear seized Sharonne and she hurried to his side with hat still carefully shielding her face, and cloak concealing all evidence of the female form beneath.

"M-My Lord Marquess! L-Let us not be too hasty, I

pray you," she entreated anew—a groan resounding from her adversary. "Surely even at this advanced hour there is yet possibility of a . . . a . . . r-re . . . con . . . cil . . . iation?"

"Reconciliation? You rally me, I think? 'S death, I warrant ye'd stand greater chance o' me being struck b' lightning!" was his contemptuous reply as he drew his sword from its scabbard with a grating rasp to test its balance.

Sharonne winced and fell trembling to her knees in a kind of obeisance, desperate to abandon the fight.

"B-But I am ready—willing—eager to apologise! Look, thus on my knees! Please, my lord, spare me! I- It will never happen again, I give you my word—"

The Marquess muttered a vehement curse. "Ecod! Ye give me nought but the melancholy! Petition your Maker, not me. You demanded satisfaction, and I'm here to see that you get it. Come! On your feet, stripling!"

And suiting action to words, he dragged Sharonne up off her knees by a handful of cloak and gave her a shove—not too gentle—in the direction of the famed Ring, the scene of many a tragic end. Thus forced to accept the inevitable, she made shift to prepare to meet her doom by discarding the cloak only, for she did not dare discard anything more and risk betrayal. Even so, she made prodigious bother of this in her endeavours to postpone her fate as long as possible. How long she would be able to befool her shrewd opponent once she was face to face with him she was loth to contemplate, likewise the savage payment he would exact from her in return for the deliberate deception. Perhaps it were better that she perish on the sword after all!

And so, with the die already cast, Sharonne rammed her hat more firmly on her head in a gesture of resignation and joined her adversary, sword in hand, with foreboding dogging her heels. The valet and surgeon stood stiffly by whilst Lord Ravenby approached the combatants to recite something—she was too dazed to determine precisely what—then he retired to throw down the handkerchief as a signal for the fight to commence.

Not daring to raise her eyes to her rival's face, Sharonne kept them rigidly trained upon his right hand which clasped the lethal weapon, the blade glinting in the first rays of the early-morning sun which now pierced the waning mist. All was electrifyingly silent except for the song of the thrush and the deafening thud of her own heart as she stood with every muscle in her slender young body taut, and her sword poised threateningly, to do exactly what, she had not the remotest idea for she had never held the weapon in her entire existence.

He seemed to be waiting an interminable time . . . was it possible he had changed his mind and would accept her apology after all? Or had he fallen asleep on his feet? No—he wasn't dead, she reluctantly admitted, as she had first hoped, for she could discern quite clearly the rise and fall of the snowy Mechlin lace beneath his chin, which was the highest point she dared manoeuvre her vision. Or perhaps he already nurtured suspicions . . . ?

Suddenly he lunged at her and Sharonne sprang back three feet into the air as if she had stepped upon a wasps' nest—a state of alarm the Marquess took full advantage of by following up with a composite attack, engaging her sword, and with a deft manipulation of his blade, completely disarmed her.

She was aghast! Bewildered! It had all happened so rapidly she had not been given a moment to think! Alas, standing thus so vulnerably exposed, her next reaction was typically female. She cowered away from him, flinging one hand across her face and the other across her bosom, awaiting the decisive blow which would despatch her to the hereafter. Through a chink in her trembling fingers she saw Lord Ashton raise the deadly blade as he towered over her, and in one fell stroke whisked the hat from her head and her shock of auburn hair cascaded down her back. Sharonne continued to keep her face averted, unable to behold the expression of fiendish rage she knew must be hovering somewhere overhead. But if my Lord Marquess was so enraged he certainly kept it admirably concealed.

"By the gods, may I be stricken with the pox if 'tis not our damsel in distress, Rave—see here! Forsooth, a determined wench an' no mistake," he purred like a lynx with its claws temporarily sheathed. "And where, an I make s' bold, is Master Stripling? Laying abed in his curl-papers, I'll be bound. Jenson!" In the two strides the valet was at his side. "Betake yourself at once to number nine Albemarle Street and summon hither a certain youth b' the name o' Falconer. Should he prove a trifle reticent, charge him that unless he appears here within the hour I shall openly debauch his sister in the most diabolical manner I can contrive! Get ye gone!"

"No! Wait!" cried out Sharonne in a sudden flash of inspiration, confronting my lord with her head held proudly erect, aware that she would probably suffer this fate whether Jonathan were protected or no. "Y-Your trouble will be in vain, for m-my brother isn't there. He's gone! Fled in the night!"

The sneer died on my lord's thin lips and his eyes narrowed suspiciously, dangerously, as the lynx finally bared its claws—the valet's powdered head shuttling from one to the other, wondering whom to obey.

It was rather unfortunate that the surgeon chose this inopportune moment to voice his unsolicited opinion.

"With all respect, Lord Ashton," he ventured cautiously, tugging at his linen stock as if he were about to expire with asphyxiation, "but do you consider such in accordance with the code, and the ethics of a gentleman?"

The Marquess repaid this presumption with a glancing blow to the medic's head, knocking his great bushy physical wig and flat wide-brimmed hat into a mud patch—before rounding on Sharonne.

"You lying jade!" he snarled, unable to credit that his quarry would have thus dared to elude him. "What gentleman of honour would abscond in such fashion leaving his sister at *my* mercy?"

"J-Jonathan would, my l-lord . . . I-I swear on my life, there's no greater craven on earth than he!" babbled she, trying to master her chattering teeth and achieve some intelligibility, as she shrank away two paces.

The Marquess stood motionless, staring back at her, smouldering with passion and white rage, yet seeming prepared to weigh the credibility of her statement.

It was at this crucial moment, when Lord Ashton was about to acknowledge this possibility, when all was hushed and the whole world seemed to hang suspended, that Sharonne first heard it, a faint cry on the gentle breeze which turned her heart to ice, accompanied by the sound of hoof-beats—both beats and cry growing gradually louder, louder.

"Sharonne! Sharonne! Where are you?"

Yes, my Lord Marquess had heard it too, for there was the malicious glean in his eye and the cynical smile on his lips, as Jonathan drew nigh.

"You were saying, mistress?" prompted Lord Ashton with blistering sarcasm before sauntering off with a burst of inane laughter to greet the new arrival—sword in hand.

'No, Jonathan! No!' Sharonne cried inwardly, willing him to go back before it was too late as she swayed beneath the impact of this devastating blow, eyes tight closed to stem the tears already pricking their lids and in a vain bid to blot out of her mind the dire consequences which were flagrantly manifest. Her efforts had all been to no avail! Jonathan had evidently woken earlier than anticipated and found his sword gone, arousing his suspicions. Further investigation would establish her boudoir empty and some of his clothing missing, after which he simply had to call at Ashton House to ascertain the time and place of venue.

"Sharonne! Sharonne!" he cried, wild-eyed and distraught, leaping from his plunging horse to dash to her side and clasp her to him in a frenzy of anxiety. "Sister! What has that savage fiend done to you? What in heaven's name possessed you to come here? Why didn't you tell me the truth?"

Meanwhile, my Lord Marquess reclined nonchalantly against a tree, his long fair hair, confined at the nape of his neck, stirring gently with the breeze as he surveyed the pathetic little scene with an air of languid amusement whilst regaling his sensitive nostrils with a few grains of snuff—his own peculiar mixture. He had not stood long thus when he was joined by Lord Ravenby, grave of visage.

"Gabriel," he besought him, deeply disturbed and unable to look his friend in the eye. "Cannot you spare the boy?"

"No, Charles," came the other's laconic response, his idle gaze meandering along the distant horizon.

"I agree he was unpardonably offensive and that it would require a man of exceptional courage to overlook such behaviour, but surely . . ."

His voice tailed off as the Marquess turned a withering eye upon him.

"Plague take ye, Charles, ye begin to grow tedious! Damn m' soul to perdition if ye didn't overture the same devious ploy only a se'nnight ago before I impaled Shadleigh to his front door."

Lord Ravenby had the grace to redden. "But consider the circumstances, Gabe. Moreover, bear in mind that I have ne'er begged anything of you before, throughout our long acquaintance."

This had never occurred to Lord Ashton and he put his head on one side, musing over the novel thought.

"As I live and breathe, I do believe you're right," he pondered, stroking his flawless cheek with a long tapering forefinger, then heaved a sigh of forlorn hope. "Alas it quite harrows me that I find m'self obliged to refuse you, for you do appreciate, do you not, that I am but a pawn in life's lamentable game? That Fate has decreed

I pluck every feather off this plump bantam cock and cut him down to size? And who am I, m' dear fellow, to say Fate nay?"

Lord Ravenby stiffened and accepted the rebuff with a curt bow.

"Forgive me, Gabriel. I, above all people, ought to have known better than to make such an appeal."

"Avast, my friend, and consider yon stripling. . . . Tell me, would you term his present demeanor apologetic?"

Lord Ravenby ceded the point and hurriedly retreated as Jonathan, demented with rage, snatched up the discarded sword and sprang at the Marquess, intending to bisect him in one fell stroke.

"Jonathan—no!" screamed Sharonne, but the Marquess deftly side-stepped and the blade sliced innocuously into the tree trunk.

With a mocking laugh Lord Ashton—a deal more nimble in shirt and breeches than Jonathan in a heavy garb—nicked three paste buttons of the latter's coat as he struggled to wrench his sword free of the tree. This humiliation did nought to sweeten Jonathan's temper and he rounded on his foe blazing with outrage, throwing fencing protocol to the wall as he hacked, cut, lunged and parried for all he was worth, but to his further discomposure not once did his weapon make contact with its target, and when next he glanced at his coat, not a solitary button remained thereon.

Next the hat was twirled from his head and the linen from his throat without as much as a scratch to his person, goading him to cry out in fury.

"Have you come to fight me or undress me, you cowardly fop?"

"Which would you prefer, stripling?" countered the mocking voice of his foe with flamboyant riposte.

"I'll teach you to seek diversion at my expense!" growled the youth, charging anew into the fray.

"Jonathan, take care!" screamed his sister more frenziedly than before, dashing across in wild appeal to Lord Ravenby.

"Stop them! Stop them! My Lord Ravenby, I implore you!"

My lord said nought but took Sharonne firmly by the arm to prevent her taking the necessary action in his stead, as she showed every intention of doing.

The sardonic curl of Lord Ashton's lip became more pronounced as he began to fight in earnest, gradually increasing pressure and pace until Jonathan's gasps were bursting from his lungs at a rate of two to the second and his sword-arm lagged as if the weapon were made of lead.

"Come, stripling, rally your strength! Heed your guard lest your breeches be next," his foe continued to gibe.

Incensed to the point of madness, Jonathan strove valiantly to whirl aloft his sword but, alas, found it hindered by something and before he could execute the vital parry, his opponent's blade pierced his heart. With his eyes bulging from his head in terror and disbelief, he staggered, spewing blood upon the fresh green grass, then fell at the Marquess's feet, quite, quite dead.

A ghastly silence pervaded the atmosphere before it was rent asunder by an ear-splitting shriek from Sharonne, who wrenched her arm free of the stricken Lord Ravenby to throw herself down prostrate by her brother's inert form, as the surgeon hastened up behind.

"J-Jon . . . ath . . . an . . . Oh—oh, J-Jon . . . ath . . . an," she sobbed, distracted with grief, unable to credit the dreadful thing which had befallen him.

Meanwhile, the Marquess stood silently by as if he had looked upon the Gorgon and suddenly turned to stone, while blood dripped from his rapier to form a small pool by his right foot.

"Gabriel!" called out his friend, three times, before he shook his head vigorously like one waking from a trance and glanced up to see Lord Ravenby hastening to his side. "Gabriel, are you all right?"

"I?" he queried with a strange laugh, plucking a handful of grass to wipe his blade clean before sheathing it. "Faith, Charles, what an incongruous question."

"Come! We must get us gone from this harrowing scene. Your man and Doctor Hoyle will do all that is necessary."

The Marquess suffered himself to be led away by Lord Ravenby who swiftly helped him to dress, and, once mounted, the two cantered out of the park, setting their steeds towards Berkeley Square, their departure not even noticed by Sharonne in this hour of tragic bereavement.

The two rode in complete silence which Lord Ravenby did not seek to disrupt until half-way up Mount Street.

"You did not truly intend killing the boy, Gabriel, I think?" he questioned rather than stated.

The Marquess rode on imperviously, his eye fixed straight ahead over the top of a flower-girl's basket.

"You are at liberty to think what you wish," was all he returned briefly.

"Do I think aright?"

Lord Ashton frowned, resenting the other's encroachment upon the hallowed ground of his personal feelings, despite their life-long association.

"Yes, damn you, Rave!"

Lord Ravenby indulged in a twisted smile. "You must exercise caution, my friend, for if I did not know you so well I'd wager you cherished a grain of human charity in that entombed heart of yours—even if it is generated by a motive of an ulterior sort. . . ."

This evoked a curious sidelong glance from the Marquess, who shrugged his ill-humour aside to reveal his customary nonchalance beneath.

"Aye, Charles, verily I'd give half my fortune for the privilege of initiating such a one at Medmenham."

"By gad! If you want her so passing well, you haven't made a very impressive start by despatching her brother to the afterlife!"

" 'Twas unfortunate," observed the Marquess in the same lackadaisical tone as he might repine the first spots of rain before a shower. "At the crucial moment when he was about to parry my thrust, alas, his blade fell foul of his coat skirts."

"She would never believe it, of course."

The Marquess heaved a sigh of futility. "Methinks you have the right of it, but mayhap by the time she's ripe for plucking she'll have forgot."

"Forgot!" Lord Ravenby manoeuvred his horse a little nearer to the Marquess as the reeking contents of a bucket descended from an upstair window on his left, splashing into the gutter nearby. "My dear Gabriel, you must appreciate that all and sundry do not rate human life as cheaply as you yourself. I vow Miss Falconer will ne'er forget—nor forgive."

Lord Ashton remained sceptical of his friend's prophecy.

"Perchance you would care to stake your new Brescia matched flintlocks?" he parried with infuriating sang-froid as they turned from Mount Street into Berkeley Square.

"Be flippant if you wish, Gabriel, nevertheless you would do well to show a modicum of healthy respect for the law, till this ugly business dies down."

"The law? But, my good fellow, 'twas an affair of honour."

"You do not need me to remind you that there are those in authority who not only consider it wilful murder, but would sacrifice ten years of their lives to see you convicted and hanged."

"What a devilish dismal dog y'are, Rave!" jeered Lord Ashton, reining to a halt at his door, to be met by a groom and two footmen. "I have witnesses to testify to mine extreme provocation. Howbeit, dear friend," he went on, favouring Lord Ravenby with his rare angelic smile and an affectionate hand on his shoulder, "I do solemnly swear to be the quintessence of discretion."

Lord Ravenby was dubiously relieved, knowing how reckless his friend could be, but doubts apparently still pervaded his peace of mind.

"I marvel, Gabriel, that you do not appear to fear recrimination from another quarter," he commented as he dismounted alongside the Marquess.

"Mistress Falconer?" exclaimed Lord Ashton with a

chuckle of incredulity as the two ascended the stairs into Ashton House. "M' dear Charles, I fear this new sentimental cult is devouring your wits! What in Satan's name should I have to fear from the female?"

What indeed!

Epilogue

OUTSIDE a fashionable residence in Pall Mall, purportedly occupied by a lady of somewhat questionable repute, a coach and four was stationed, the coachman slouched upon his box, two parts dozing and three parts intoxicated, as he languished alongside his slumbering liveried companion hour upon dreary hour, awaiting his master's convenience.

With monotonous regularity he drew a flask from one capacious pocket of his triple-caped wrap-rascal, from which he sought to extract yet another droplet of comforting spirit, but this had long since coursed its way down his hoarse throat. Apart from the flambeau ensconced high upon the wall of the house and the dim coach-lantern, the street was cloaked in darkness, for it was but three in the morn—suddenly verified by the watch whose strident call and grating rattle sounded about two streets distant as he passed on his laborious round.

To all appearances the coachman and postilion would seem to be the sole inhabitants of the street, and well might their *naïveté* be excused in so believing at such an hour. However, if one peered more closely into the murky blackness to their rear, a ragged unkempt figure may possibly have been detected creeping stealthily upon the two—then another, and another, making three in all, and each clutching cudgels of substantial proportions in their calloused hands, their intent evidently of an evil nature. A common enough occurrence in London of the eighteenth century, but what three such felonious rascals hoped to acquire from the simple menials remained to be seen. Needless to say, the two stayed oblivious to the lurking danger until they were brutally assaulted and laid unconscious with swift heavy blows to their skulls, following which they were dragged bodily off into the shadows.

The three rogues were gone but a minute when they returned to assume position upon the coachbox, one at the fore clad in the coachman's great coat and hat, obscuring his eyes, whilst his companions skulked at the back, relying upon the darkness to preserve their anonymity. They remained thus almost an hour when the night stillness was shattered by a loud bang as the door of the house burst wide, allowing the uproarious merriment from the Baccanalian festivities within to pervade the outer atmosphere, and the blinding light from the brilliantly lit hall to streak across the roadway, prompting the three impostors to submerge their misshapen faces another two inches inside the confines of their turned-up collars. But they had little to fear, for the owner of the conveyance was in no state of sobriety to identify even an orang-utan upon the box as he staggered and stumbled down the steps of the house and up the steps of the coach. Once his recumbent body was sprawled inside, the 'coachman' leaned across and slammed the door, whipped up the team and the vehicle lurched off, though unbeknownst to the inebriated gentleman, in a direction which ran counter to his inclination. One might suppose he had passed into oblivion, however, for it was not until the conveyance had traversed the length of London and was descending, with a deal of jolting and bumping, the narrow squalid streets of Wapping towards the lower reaches of the Thames, that the occupant began to sense that perhaps all was not quite as well as it ought to be and so voiced his protests in the Billingsgate vernacular. At the same time the coach rumbled to a halt in the lowest quarter of the city, where rats, filth and stench were to be found in plenty by the fetid river, and the coach-lanterns were the only lights to permeate the inky darkness for miles around.

No sooner had the equipage stopped than the gentleman flung open the door and thrust out indignant head to repeat his objection in more sonorous and abusive terms, when a brutal blow descended from a heavy cudgel, and he crumpled to the muddy ground, silenced for some considerable while.

This seemed to encourage great haste as two of the men hauled the victim up and the third stepped up to a small door concealed in the shadows to give three long knocks followed by two short. Almost immediately the door creaked ajar, letting escape a thin stream of light —not sufficient to illuminate the fourth conspirator who, in any case, was enveloped from head to toe in a black voluminous hooded cloak—and enough room for the two men to bear their inert load inside, whilst the first man returned to the coach and drove off again into the night as the door of the hovel closed upon his accomplices.

If the air was considered obnoxious outside it was nevertheless mild compared to that within the dingy domicile which, in fact, was little more than a damp covered hole, furnished only with an abundance of dirty straw and a wooden box, upon which an oil lamp exuded turbid fumes which did nought to enhance the atmosphere.

Upon the straw in one corner lay the supine form of the Most Honourable Marquess of Ashton, resplendent in all his finery, and his blond silken hair forming a gleaming halo round his pale delicately handsome features, whilst the three stood over him in silence—the two men evidently awaiting further instructions from the mysterious cloaked figure, who was also heavily veiled.

"You know what you must do?"—the voice was that of a woman.

The two nodded and grunted confirmation, tugging a forelock.

"Very well," she resumed, stepping over the straw towards a narrow aperture in the wall, sending rats and mice scampering to their holes. "Do it quickly and quietly. I shall return anon." And with that she disappeared into the adjacent room

Some minutes later she returned, bearing a bowl of dark fluid and a cloth, to find the Marquess stripped of his fashionable elegance and clad in the filthy coarse rags of a scavenger, the sight of which seemed to please her.

"Good," she approved. "You have worked well. You took care to besmirch his fair skin? We do not want it arousing curiosity."

She received their mumbled acknowledgment, then drew forth a pair of silver scissors from her underpocket and set to work on his lordship's long tresses. Not until his head was completely shorn did she return the scissors to her pocket and take up the bowl and cloth, whilst her helpmates gazed on dumbfounded yet somewhat anxious, if the way they cast intermittent glances over their shoulders was aught to go by, as if half expecting the devil himself to come to rescue this his loyal servant in his moment of need.

But the female suffered no such qualms as she continued assiduously in her ministrations, ensuring that every inch of my lord's visible flesh and hair was stained with the walnut juice, until she finally relinquished her task, satisfied that even his own valet should not recognise him. But as she straightened up, the Marquess stirred, emitting a groan, prompting the three to draw in their breath and exchange warning glances.

"Make haste!" commanded the female. "Bring the gin hither."

No sooner was the order given than one of the felons produced a large stone jar from which emanated the eye-watering effluvium of the cheapest gin, the very smell of which seemed guaranteed to shrivel the liver to the size and context of a prune. This was applied liberally to my lord's garments and person and the remainder poured down his throat by one man whilst the other pinioned his arms lest he struggle.

Again the woman was obviously pleased and, as before, commended her hirelings—who left the prisoner gasping and wheezing as if the spirit were corroding his very lungs.

However, it was at this precise moment that a faint cry was to be heard outside, of a raucous voice but at a distance, which urged the woman to raise a gloved hand aloft in a gesture of silence.

"Hark! I believe they come at last."

All three listened intently and the cry came again, a little nearer, near enough to distinguish the words, in fact.

"Come, all ye fine able-bodied men! Who will take up the King's shilling and join us aboard his ship the *Challenge*, bound for the Americas on the morning tide? Who will serve King and country?"

The *Challenge*! Even the name of the vessel seemed portentous.

Thus, Gabriel Francis Louis Philippe St Claire, fourth Marquess of Ashton, disappeared without trace. As it was rumoured that my lord had killed his man in yet another duel, society at large assumed him to have evacuated the London scene until the hue and cry had died down—for why should anyone privileged to belong to this elevated circle suspect the remotest connection betwixt the fastidious leader of fashion and the new seemingly intoxicated recruit in labourer's garb with cropped dark head and reeking like a drunken dunghill in midsummer who had been smuggled aboard His Majesty's ship *Challenge* that very morn?

PART TWO

1

SEVEN years had lapsed since the fateful duel, during which nought whatsoever was seen or heard of the Marquess of Ashton, and Sharonne blossomed into the accomplished beauty predicted by her father. Consequently, she was an instant success upon her presentation to society at the age of seventeen, and throughout the subsequent years, despite her disparity of fortune, did not lack for offers of marriage, some highly advantageous, and some not so advantageous. But advantageous or no, whether rich, handsome or titled—or even all three—Sharonne had no compunction in spurning them at every turn, and soon earned a reputation as a female of somewhat fickle disposition, unable to make up her mind, and rather than confer her favours upon one admirer preferred to scatter them at random amongst them all.

Not surprisingly, she had long become the despair of her doting parents—and even Aunt Matilda, who had recently made it known that she would cut her niece off without the proverbial shilling if she did not accept the next gentleman to declare himself. And it certainly did nothing to enhance her chances, the venerable lady was heard to deprecate, by giving licence to her defiant spirit and staring the gentlemen disconcertingly out of countenance! But despite Aunt Matilda's dire threat, Sharonne continued to reject her swains in gay abandon until her parents and aunt had relinquished all hope.

Each month throughout the Season Sharonne's engagement diary was full to capacity, and the month of May was no exception. Upon the fifteenth she was invited to attend a ridotto at no less a place than Northumberland House in company with her mamma but which the latter felt obliged to politely decline on account of her vapours going to her brain. Loath to disappoint her daughter, she suggested Sharonne attend the function with a certain Lady Benton who also was privileged to receive an invitation, a lady of punctilious standards and beneath whose viligant eye Sharonne's unblemished reputation would be sure to remain inviolate.

For the occasion Sharonne spared no pains with her toilette, hoping as she never ceased to hope that this time her efforts would not be in vain, that she would meet the man she was destined to love to eternity and for whom she would willingly fling herself into Rosamund's Pond, for despite what everyone else thought, no one was more disconsolate than she at finding herself obliged to continuously reject her suitors. However, nothing was more repugnant to her than the prospect of a marriage of convenience, and if she could possibly combine love and riches as the Gunning girls had done, life should prove so much more agreeable. Nevertheless, thus far Cupid's arrow had failed to pierce her impervious heart and she had to admit that her hopes were beginning to fray a trifle round the edges, along with those of her relatives.

To attend the ridotto Aunt Matilda had furnished her rather handsomely with a magnificent new gown, thereby hoping to attract every eligible male present to her niece's feet, trusting by the law of averages that she was bound to develop a tendre for *one* of them. The gown was a billowing *robe à l'anglaise* in the palest of pink muslins and the height of mode, with treble lace flounces at the elbows and a bodice cut provocatively low to display her voluptuous curves to advantage—as Aunt Matilda intended it should—and worn over a star-spangled petticoat and substantial hoops. The train was fashionably long, and which Sharonne manoeuvred with all the finesse of her six years' experience in the *Beau Monde*. And having been closeted with her maid for three full hours being powdered, perfumed and duly patched upon the most alluring, though visible, parts of her anatomy, the final result was one of poetic perfection. She bestowed one last glance in her looking-glass and smiled, fingering the long powdered ringlet caressing her right shoulder, well pleased with the result.

But alas, at Northumberland House there was no different tale to be told, for Sharonne suffered disappointment upon disappointment to find not a solitary new eligible face amongst the distinguished throng, apart from a certain Mr Boswell newly arrived from Scotland who did not appeal to her taste. All the familiar families adorned in the conventional—though extremely fashionable—gowns and full-skirted coats of satin and brocade, glittering with brilliants and the various orders according to their rank, all flashing and sparkling beneath the ponderous crystal chandeliers as the cream of Society stepped a lively contradanse, promenaded in the minstrels' gallery, perspired over the gaming tables, flirted outrageously, or simply sat by the side observing, with a painstakingly cultivated air of boredom, the antics of their intimates.

At present Sharonne fell into the last category, having grown wearied of dancing and not a little deflated by the sameness of it all, for she may well have been seated thus at the Duchess of Bedford's rout last week —or my Lady Harrington's ball the week before. Everything and everyone all exactly the same—but wait! What was that? Something unusual, something dark, very dark, caught her eye of a sudden—a dark head, which could scarce pass unnoticed against the background of powered wigs, predominantly white wigs with a spattering of pastel shades, pinks and blues—but none of black!

She craned her neck in a variety of positions the better to investigate the strange phenomenon, but it had gone.

"Something amiss, my dear?" questioned Lady Benton, elevating her ear-trumpet a little higher and who, seated next to her charge, was loath to miss anything.

"N-No, your ladyship," stammered Sharonne, sitting back in her plush upholstered chair of gilded beechwood. "I merely thought I spied an old acquaintance."

This satisfied the matronly lady and no more was said, but Sharonne's wide eyes continued to rake the gathering—though as furtively as possible—for further sight of the dark head. Yes! There it was again amongst the dancers—she was able to get a much better view this time. It was a man! Well, she thought it might be sporting, as he did, a short black beard and moustache, but certainly not one so dark. Definitely not English by all appearances, with such black crisp curling hair, worn short as a Spaniard probably would. Yes, decidedly Spanish, thought she, regarding him curiously, and with more than his fair share of the passion peculiar to his race, judging by the manner in which he was slyly kissing his partner's hand each time he took it, and dancing much, much closer to her than convention decreed, despite the magnitude of her hoop-petticoat! And heaven alone knew what he was whispering in her delicate pink ear to make her giggle and flush up to the roots of her powdered hair.

Something very akin to jealousy was slowly consuming Sharonne and not having experienced the emotion before she was quite unable to put a name to it. Even so, it was an emotion she did not relish. Her eager eyes continued to follow the fascinating 'Spaniard' whenever possible, clinging to him and his attractive partner like ivy to a damp wall, as she responded to Lady Benton's small talk with half-hearted monosyllables.

It was with a feeling of some relief that Sharonne watched the dance end and the 'Spaniard' return his partner to her chair, retiring from her side with a final kiss upon her dainty hand and which seemed to cling to his a little too long as if she were loath to let him go, thought Sharonne—or was it pure conjecture?

Her eyes again followed him as he swaggered across the floor; the whaleboned skirts of his magnificent coat of silver stuff swinging rhythmically as he progressed with all the confidence and audacity of one adored by the ladies and cursed by the gentlemen, when he was pounced upon by his charming hostess, the Countess of Northumberland, whose spouse was deeply engrossed in steep play at the card-tables, and so felt at liberty to flirt to her heart's content with her male guests, rapping her Don Juan over the arm with her fan of painted vellum in response to his repartee, and simpering like a young girl in receipt of her first compliment.

Yes, he was evidently someone of great importance,

but who? This Sharonne simply had to establish at all cost ere the night was out or she would never be privileged to enjoy another peaceful sleep again as long as she lived!

The Countess finally whisked away as a musical diversion was announced and the 'Spaniard' availed himself of a seat not too far distant from Sharonne herself, close enough, in fact, for her to determine the colour and nature of his eyes—when she dared to glance his way.

Suddenly it happened! Their eyes met! Sharonne drew in her breath with a loud gasp and immediately glanced away, her heart pounding like the hooves of a runaway horse.

"Something amiss, my dear?" enquired Lady Benton again, which would appear to be her standard phrase.

"Er—n-nothing at all, your ladyship," replied Sharonne as before, wildly conscious of the stranger's disconcerting gaze still upon her. "I—I merely find the room a trifle warm."

And in evidence of this she threw open her fan and proceeded to flap it vigorously over her heaving bosom in time to the lively finale of the Vivaldi Concerto being performed.

Passionate, just as she suspected! Eyes of bright blue with a blazing passion lurking in their mysterious depths! What chance of survival did a poor defenceless female have 'neath the influence of such?

It was some appreciable time before Sharonne could venture another look at her 'Spaniard', and when she did, found his attention to be absorbed elsewhere, and breathed a little easier. As her hand was committed to the Honourable Richard Dalrymple for the quadrille which followed, she was obliged to postpone her analysis of the stranger until a more convenient moment.

But here she erred, for upon assuming her position in the line of dancers whom should she find standing adjacent to Mr Dalrymple but the audacious stranger, staring across at her in what could only be termed a look of barefaced seduction! Despite her twenty-three years, never had she been overcome with such confusion and embarrassment—nor unmitigated delight, could she but persuade herself to confess it. Instinctively her right hand progressed to the ribboned knots adorning her stomacher to still her heart which again rebelled against all efforts to control it, leaving her quite breathless before the dance was even begun. All the same, Sharonne could not own herself anything but frantic with glee! He had actually noticed her, was attracted to her! What ought she to do next to secure his regard?

Nothing! It was evident that 'Don Juan' had the operation well under control, for upon reaching out her hand to her partner it was unexpectedly taken in a strong vibrant clasp—certainly not that of Richard—and glancing up Sharonne gasped again to find her hand in the stranger's possession as he deftly usurped Mr Dalrymple's place. Was there no end to the fellow's presumption, wondered she, though secretly applauding the clever manoeuvre about which Richard was able to do little except acknowledge Miss Elinor Fothersley as his new partner.

Sharonne may have felt urged to make some comment had not she been bereft of words. To be observed dancing thus with this absolute stranger would be termed most indiscreet. Even if she did have little say in the matter, she doubted exceedingly if Lady Benton would view it that way.

Her new partner made no attempt to converse. He did not need to, for his eyes made his meaning abundantly clear as he brushed the back of her hand with his lips, sending a shock-wave reverberating through her body, which he was bound to sense for it shot right through to her fingertips!

Sharonne was not allowed to recover from this before she felt his kiss on the palm of her hand—then the nape of her neck as she turned, graduating to her protruding left shoulder! Where next? she asked herself, battling to ignore the thrills leap-frogging up and down her spine and focus her mind on the dance. The man was dangerous—frighteningly so! Such an one might demand aught he wished of her and she would be utterly powerless to say him nay.

Indeed, if Cupid in capricious mood could generate love at first sight, then Sharonne should prove a classic example, for if her partner had deigned to overture a proposal of marriage at the end of the quadrille she would have accepted him there and then without any compunction whatsoever. But he did not. Instead, he was the quintessence of gentlemanly conduct as he bowed low over her hand then gallantly escorted her back to her chair by Lady Benton—still with never a word passing between them.

Howbeit, this shocking breach of etiquette Lady Northumberland could not allow beneath her own roof and she at once swept across to rectify the omission.

"Edmund! I vow you are an incorrigible rogue," she chided him playfully. "To commence the dance with one female and end it with another, I do declare you surpass even yourself. Fie on you, for snatching the hearts of two innocent doves from under my very nose!"

"I stand rebuked, ma'am," smiled he disarmingly, with a flash of gleaming white teeth. "But as heaven's my witness, 'tis such a veritable age since I hath trod a measure that I'm afraid I quite mistook the way of it. Mayhap, you would deign to spare me an hour or two to correct mine erring feet?"

'English! He was English!' Sharonne enthused inwardly.

"La! 'Tis not your feet which stand in need of correction, you handsome rake, as you very well know," went on the Countess with a significant nod in Sharonne's direction, evoking a boyish grin from her debonair guest and a fierce blush to Sharonne's cheeks as she stood self-consciously twisting her fingers into knots on her ladyship's nether side. "Sharonne, my love," my lady addressed her amiably, "I appreciate 'tis somewhat belated, nevertheless, you must allow me to present you without more ado to this gentleman who, I give you fair warning, would have your feet erring alongside his own, yet who has but newly arrived in England to swell the ranks of society's most eligible bachelors."

Having enunciated this with all the grace and elegance at her command, the Countess then turned to the gentleman.

"Edmund, permit me to present to you, Miss Sharonne Falconer, only daughter of Sir Giles and Lady Falconer of Hertfordshire, and, I might add, one of our most outstanding beauties—not that you need to be told!" She then turned back to Sharonne as the gentleman swept a magnificent leg. "Sharonne, pray make your curtsy to Edmund St Claire, Marquess of Ashton."

In response, Sharonne did a rather surprising thing. She sank deep within the confines of her billowing hoop-petticoats, not in the decorous curtsy anticipated, but in a dead faint!

2

SHARONNE drifted slowly back into the conscious world to the urgent reiteration of her name, accompanied by a general hubbub of voices and the ethereal strains of a minuet. And as feeling returned to her being she became aware of someone chafing vigorously at her left hand. Suddenly a pungent odour assaulted her nostrils, completely taking her breath away and causing her to cough and splutter rather unbecomingly.

The odour disappeared to be replaced by the hysterical voice of Lady Benton, drawing the attention of all and sundry to the fact that 'Sharonne is recovering at last!'

Blinking open her eyes, she gazed up into a hazy snowstorm of black and white flakes floating hither and thither until they gradually settled upon the dark head of the gentleman and the white powdered heads of her hostess and Lady Benton.

"Sharonne, child, do you feel well?" queried Lady Northumberland, anxiously fluttering her fan over her prone guest. "I do declare, you did quite overset us all."

"I vow she has been insensible a full ten minutes or more!" asseverated Lady Benton, giving every indication of swooning away in sympathy as she urgently applied the aromatic bottle to her own, pinched nostrils.

Sharonne hurriedly struggled into a sitting posture from her prostration upon the velvet settee, ready to sink with mortification beneath the gentleman's intense regard.

"P-Please forgive me—I—I apologise most p-pro-foundly," she stammered, rattling her brains for a plausible reason for making such a fool of herself in order to divert any astute mind present from the true one. "I —I really cannot say what possessed me to do such a silly thing. It must surely be the stifling heat."

"Mayhap, when you are sufficiently recovered, Miss Falconer, you would care to adjourn to the gardens for a breath of air?" volunteered my Lord Ashton. "I should deem myself honoured if you would permit me to escort you hence."

Sharonne's immediate instinct warned her to refuse his courteous offer for it was quite obvious that who-ever he was he most certainly was *not* the Marquess of Ashton, and therefore an impostor. But if she were to reject his offer out of hand she may not be granted an-other such opportunity to discover precisely who he was and what kind of chicanery he was about. Further-more, if she chose to own it, her heart and every sense in her body were urging her to go for reasons quite alien to the dictates of her head, and so the former won.

However, if Sharonne considered Lord Ashton's mo-tive gravely suspect, so too did Lady Benton who lost no time in voicing her objection—to be graciously but firmly countermanded by her hostess who assured her that little could go amiss, even in the company of my Lord Ashton, in the brief spell it would take to inhale a lungful or two of air.

No sooner were they out of the congested ballroom and under the stars than my lord cast the façade of the gay cavalier from him like a cloak. It was not anything he said or did in particular which transformed Sharonne's opinion but something she sensed in his attitude, or was it her own deep-rooted guilt?

"Who are you, sir?" queried she with candour, thereby hoping he might choose to repay her in like manner.

He returned a blank stare. "Who else but the Marquess of Ashton, ma'am, as our hostess informed you."

Sharonne pulled up short to round on him, all the signs of profound emotional disturbance physically manifest.

"How can you be, when I know the Marquess to be as fair as you are dark? As sinister and ruthless as you are warm-hearted and generous? As frigid as you are passionate? And, in general, as inhuman as you are human!"

"By the faith, Miss Falconer, you paint a very fitting portrait of brother Gabriel!"

Sharonne gaped in astonishment. "Y-Your brother? H-He is your brother?" she stuttered stupidly, unable to absorb the fact for some reason that these two diverse characters could be in any wise related. "I—I didn't know he had a b-brother."

"No, ma'am, not many people do, due to a family estrangement," he responded imperturbably. "But I hear tell your family too is estranged from the St Claires."

"Y-Yes," was all she chose to say as they resumed their perambulations along the paved terrace.

"Alas, a failing of brother Gabriel, I'm afraid," he sighed ruefully. "He seemed determined to make enemies where'er he went."

His lapse into the past tense prompted her next question, and her eagerness to discover exactly how much he knew.

"Do you have any intelligence concerning your brother and what has befallen him?"

"In what way, Miss Falconer?" he parried swiftly.

Sharonne drew herself up sharply and made haste to cover her blunder.

"It is widely rumoured, sir, that he disappeared in very mysterious circumstances."

"Aye," he murmured with an air of futility—or indifference. "I thought you may be able to enlighten me in some way."

"My lord, your tone would seem to imply that you know even less than I?" she probed, striving to suppress the urgency in her voice.

"No more than my Lord Ravenby either, who was his closest friend. Vanished in the night without trace, I understand. Of course, there are those—like I myself—who believe he was set upon by footpads, stripped and robbed, for his clothing and personal belongings were subsequently found in pawnbrokers all over London, not to mention his coach left abandoned." He meandered on, stroking his beard meditatively. "Strange, is it not, Miss Falconer, how his body was ne'er discovered? And why you should swoon at the very mention of his name?"

Sharonne thought she was about to do so again. "N-No, sir, I—I swear, I was overcome by—"

"Do not fence with me, mistress." Was the choice of phrase deliberate? "If you suffocated with the heat, then why was your hand as cold as a pauper's grave? And why did you tremble so—as you do now?"

Sharonne's countenance was redeemed by a flunkey

in the Northumberland livery who appeared most opportunely bearing a glass of cordial upon a silver salver, which he presented to her with his mistress's compliments. Sharonne conveyed her thanks for her hostess's kind consideration and raised the glass at once to her lips to choke upon the first gulp, for the cordial was generously laced with brandy. An admirable way to guarantee a merry evening, thought she, regulating her gulps to genteel sips. However, the 'cordial', coupled with the knowledge that her companion was evidently in ignorance concerning his brother's true fate, pervaded her with an element of relief. How could he possibly ascertain more than she was foolish enough to divulge?

He smiled cryptically as he guided her across to a long rustic garden seat, positioned by the stone balustrade bordering the terrace, which linked twin flights of stairs leading down into the gardens.

"But I forget, ma'am," he resumed affably. "You have reason to despise my brother's memory almost as much as I."

He was certainly well informed, acknowledged she —nevertheless rejoicing inwardly at the news, for if he truly despised his brother to such extent he may be inclined to view her heinous secret with leniency, should he happen to discover all, and perhaps even rejoice along with her and regard her as some kind of dubious benefactor in assisting his accession to the Ashton title and all it entailed.

As she was not going to be drawn out and so enlighten him, he took it upon himself to enlighten her.

"I am given to understand by my Lord Ravenby that there took place a duel—"

"Please! I beg you, say no more! The recollection is too painful."

"A thousand pardens, Miss Falconer! My conscience could ne'er endure the anguish of distressing a lady," he petitioned her, availing himself of her hand to raise it to his lips. "Especially one so breathtakingly beautiful. I would merely express my sincere trust that my brother's indiscretion will not thwart our better acquaintance."

"I see no reason why it should," she replied encouragingly, making provocative play with eyelashes and fan.

"As he is now presumed to be dead, I have returned to England as the dutiful prodigal to assume the title and family responsibilities."

"Are you a military man?"

Sharonne did not know why she should ask this, for he certainly gave no indication of being a soldier, and she had never, to her knowledge, seen one sporting a beard.

"I resigned my commission in the cavalry some years agone," he overtured readily, "and have subsequently lived in the East Indies."

"I see," accorded she, inwardly debating what she ought to say next to maintain a decorous level of discourse, for she could feel his eyes—barely a foot away—boring into her being with that same passion she had witnessed during the dance, and although it perturbed her somewhat to think what he might do, it perturbed her even more to think how she might reciprocate! As no man had ever had such an effect upon her before, she was quite at a loss to know what action to take when common sense and conscience were urging her to hie hence indoors whilst every other human instinct in her entire body was willing her to stay and brave his ardour.

He was a St Claire! She must resist him at all cost, for although she may deem her brother's death avenged and so be prepared to declare a truce with the St Claires, her family certainly would not.

And yet she chose to linger, her eyes flitting everywhere but in his direction as the lengthy silence took on a pregnant meaning. Her mind was a sudden blank, and so she seized upon the cordial in her hand to safeguard her honour and lingered over each sip as if it were her last, on the assumption that he would hardly feel inspired to kiss her with a wineglass adhered to her lips.

But the more Sharonne battled to resist him the more she weakened, for how could she prevent him kissing and fondling her hand, her cheek, when she was subconsciously willing him to do it?

"Sharonne," he whispered in her ear, and she almost dissolved. "I pray you will not suffer my name to come between us?"

She sat up with a start, rallying her resources whilst nervously fidgeting with the wineglass—alas, now empty—until he gently but firmly disengaged it from her trembling fingers and placed it upon the balustrade. Even the very atmosphere seemed to be against her, which could not have been more conducive to amorous intrigue, with the stars twinkling overhead and the mild breeze wafting the intoxicating fragrance of the roses about them.

"Y-You are a M-Montague . . . L-Lord Ashton, a-and I . . . a . . . a C-Capulet," she stammered, aware of nought but the disturbing fact that he was manoeuvring still nearer.

"Then are not we destined to re-enact the greatest love story ever penned?"

How she came to be enveloped in his arms was something Sharonne would never know. Her heart pounded, and the blood swirled so madly in her veins that she was quite unable to protest—had she even wished to! All she was suddenly aware of was his eyes, firing, searing her own. Burning into her very soul with a passion so intense that she could feel him overpowering her, mesmerising her, compelling her to forget who she was, who he was, and relinquish herself utterly to his will.

Here was no fumbling yokel. No, here was a skilled seducer of women, one accomplished in the amorous arts and endowed with such a plausible tongue that he would charm himself out of the very bowels of Hades. Each overture, gesture, with the experience of many conquests, was carefully premeditated ere it was bestowed—even the tone of his voice was modulated to a soft caress to compliment his actions.

"Sharonne, I find you a challenge, and no virile male can resist a challenge! I wonder why, at three-and-twenty, you are still unwed despite your captivating beauty, and discover that you cannot wed because you cannot love. This I refuse to believe, for you glance at me and I see a dormant emotion stirring in your bewitching eyes, awakening! I dance with you and I find you exuding love from every pore of your voluptuous flesh—"

"Stop! N-No . . . p-please . . . E-Edmund . . ." she tried to protest but failed lamentably.

"If thou wouldst stay me, then pray why dost thou cling to me so avidly?" he parried, unrelenting, his lips tracing their steady course along her jaw, beneath her left ear, and on down her pulsating neck . . . shoulder . . . to culminate at the alluring swell of her left breast.

"Ed . . . m-mund . . ." she gasped, floundering in a sea of delirium. "W-We have . . . not been acquain . . . ted one . . . hour. . . ."

"How long wouldst thou have? How long doth it take to acknowledge the inevitable?"

Sharonne emitted a groan of helpless ecstasy. Granted, she may be well versed in the ethics of modern society, able to acquit herself admirably at the keyboard or embroidery frame, even the cards, and had no difficulty in discouraging young beaux from taking liberties with her person—but this occasion was quite different. This time, she ashamedly admitted, she was actually wanting the gentleman to take liberties, though what Lady Benton should have thought of the admission her head was fortunately too befuddled to reason.

"I too am difficult to please," he resumed in the same velvet tone. "For many long years have I travelled the world seeking vainly the perfect woman. But at last I've found her, and I do not intend to let her go."

He kissed her once, twice, and after the third Sharonne was his unto death!

"Sharonne," he breathed softly—ever so softly. "Could you love me, mayhap?"

"Yes! Yes!" she cried out eagerly, craving his lips anew—which he now chose to deny her.

"Would you wed me, in truth, and come away with me to my country home in Dorsetshire?"

"Yes! Yes! Anything!"

102

He drew back, eyeing her with scepticism. "You would not cavil at bearing the name of St Claire?"

"No! Er—yes!"

The magic aura was shattered by the sound of the name which struck more dread into her heart than even that of Beelzebub. How could she spend the rest of her life cursed with the name of Jonathan's executioner? How would she ever reconcile her conscience? Or endure the humiliation and reproach of her loved ones? True, the man by her side may be exonerated from all blame, but she could hardly expect her parents to regard him so. And what of the burden which weighed heaviest of all—not *her* brother's death, but *his* brother's? Would not the ghost of Gabriel St Claire continue to haunt them until she could bring herself to confess all? No, this she could not contemplate at present whilst her friendship with Edmund was little more than an embryo, for although she had fallen deeply in love with him it would take a while longer to establish the implicit trust she would need to unburden her terrible secret. Obviously, she hoped that he would anon cherish enough love in his heart to be able to forgive her, but should he not, what then? What would be the dreadful alternative?

One glance at the look of horror registered on her face and the Marquess had his answer.

"I-I'm sorry," he declared hoarsely. "I ought not to have pressed you at such a time . . . taken such unfair advantage."

He would have released her, but she clung to his arm, loath to let him go.

"Please, Edmund," she besought him in earnest. "Y-You misunderstand, it's not what you think! I love you beyond any doubt, despite our brief acquaintance, and would wed you this very night! But I need a little time . . . m-my parents would disapprove of our union in the strongest terms."

He gently prised her rigid fingers from his huge bejewelled cuff and kissed their tips, an enigmatic smile curling his lips.

"Fret not, sweet Sharonne, I understand well enough. You must forgive me. Mine existence has been somewhat rough o'er the past years. I'm afraid I am become a creature of impulse, seizing opportunity whene'er it doth arise—quite often where none exists! I makc no secret of the fact that I came to England also to seek a wife—you, Sharonne. You are the woman I would have. And I am loath to see you quit my sight lest you vanish into the thick black London smoke, lost to me for ever."

"No! No, Edmund! I give you my promise on sacred oath, I am yours eternally—I shall never love anyone but you! N-Nonetheless . . . I—"

"Think me not a petty rogue! You need time to consider, and you shall have it! One month from this very day—"

"A month! A whole dreary month! I don't need a month, Edmund. A few days will suffice."

"Nevertheless, I shall be gone out of London for a month at least."

She stared aghast up into his handsome face, as if he had predicted the end of the world.

"G-Gone?" she faltered pitifully. "Y-You are going away? L-Leaving me so soon?"

"Alas, child, I needs must—"

"Oh, Edmund, I couldn't bear it! I—I need you, my courage will evaporate if you go now!"

"Believe me, dear one, I am equally loath to tear myself away from your side, but I must set my house in order to receive you." He rose to his feet with an air of finality and took her by the hand. "Come, Miss Falconer, 'tis time we retraced our steps within—er—if your lungs have imbibed the balmy night air to their abundant satisfaction. I fear, I spy my Lady Benton's punctilious eye focused upon us from yonder window."

Sharonne rose reluctantly afoot, following his indication to the long windows blazing forth the lights from the glittering ballroom where, sure enough, the unmistakable cottage-loaf shape of Lady Benton stood silhouetted, labouring 'neath the ostrich-like delusion that because she was unable to discern the guilty pair, they likewise were unable to see her—until my lord sketched her a most condescending bow, when she disappeard quicker than a squirrel up an oak tree.

However, as Sharonne was about to step back inside, Lord Ashton suddenly chose to detain her.

"Do not despair, sweetheart," he encouraged her with a reassuring kiss on her crestfallen cheek. "Never fear, I shall return—perchance, when you least expect."

A subtle ploy on my lord's part, who would indeed seem to understand the incongruities of the female mind, for if he nurtured any doubts concerning Sharonne's sincerity of heart, the knowledge that he was to immediately desert her could not have thrown her more decisively into his arms.

3

SHARONNE'S immediate impulse was to divulge the whole to her parents and suffer the full blast of their justifiable wrath, though not perhaps entirely justified, for her dearest Edmund was but an innocent pawn in the dastardly game, who had the direst misfortune to bear the St Claire name and be brother to her family's bitterest enemy. Why then should they wish to unreasonably persecute him as if he, and not his wicked brother, had been instrument in Jonathan's death?

However, day quickly succeeded day and ere long the time allotted by Edmund St Claire had expired, yet Sharonne still had not summoned sufficient courage to break the news to her parents. Possibly just as well as it chanced, for her Romeo did not return at the end of that month, nor the month after. In fact, he had not appeared by the end of the Season, by which time Sharonne's hopes of ever uniting in holy wedlock with the man she loved were sorely waning. Moreover, she was beginning to think the whole incident at Northumberland House as something conjured up in her overactive imagination, for now, three months later, it all savoured of fantasy, and the more time that lapsed the more fantastic it all became—that is, all except the agony consuming her heart for love of the elusive Edmund St Claire.

In desperation she prevailed week after dreary week upon her parents to linger in London, in the faint hope that Edmund would yet come to claim her hand, though her parents were given not the slightest intimation of the true reason for the delay. Nevertheless, the sad day finally dawned when the last carriage rattled off into the country and Sharonne was compelled to admit defeat and acknowledge the reality staring her starkly in the face. Edmund would never come back! He had deserted her for another, and she would never ever see him again. . . .

Sir Giles and Lady Falconer should have been blind indeed not to have observed the transformation in their offspring long ere this, for Sharonne had always exuded a tremendous zest for living, a wild exuberance with which she infected all around her. Never, in all her years as her mother, had her ladyship known her daughter weep and languish in such manner, which would seem to indicate, without any doubt, a malady of the heart. Yes, Sharonne was undeniably in love.

One need hardly say that her parents were secretly overjoyed at this and even Sir Giles was persuaded to applaud dear Matilda's brilliant strategem in purchasing the new gown, for it certainly appeared to have effected the long-desired miracle. Of course, the Falconers could not revel thus in the news for long without waxing curious about the mysterious object of their daughter's heart, although they were unanimous in the belief that he must surely be someone of exceptional qualities to have succeeded where so many young bucks had fallen by the wayside. But despite the exploitation of every conceivable means at her disposal, her ladyship's assiduous efforts to discover the identity of the strange amour failed dismally.

And so the Falconers returned to their Hertfordshire home where, once established, Sharonne sought to relieve the anguish in her heart by indulging in frequent lengthy walks through the meadows and fields which constituted her father's land. Here, in the peaceful solitude of nature's sanctuary, she was able to unburden her grief to the birds, trees and flowers—and any other living thing which cared to hearken.

It was one afternoon upon returning from such a walk that she was greeted at the door by her mother who was almost hysterical with excitement as she hustled her daughter into the house, clucking like a hen round her first batch of chicks.

"Come, girl! Make haste! Make haste! Where on earth have you been this age? Get you hence and tidy your hair! Change your gown—the blue taffety, I think —er—no, perhaps the apple-green muslin is more becoming—yes! And the pearls your father gave you when you came of age. Go quickly! The maids are waiting to attend you!"

"Dearest Mamma, do calm yourself," urged her daughter, taken appreciably aback. "What has happened? Is the world to come to an end?"

"Saucy chit! No indeed, but it may very well do so if you do not present yourself in the parlour looking your level best in five minutes!" rebuked her parent in no uncertain terms, propelling Sharonne in the direction of the stairs. "Do not goggle at me, child, as if I'd grown another head! 'Tis not every day of the week that Mr Washbourne calls!"

"Washbourne?" queried Sharonne, understandably puzzled, for it was the first time she had ever heard the name.

"Lud, girl, have you mislaid your wits? Your father and I know all about your silly game—you and your

Mr Washbourne. We are well aware of what's been going on during the past weeks. See, you blush with shame! We have watched you moping and repining over him—"

"Over whom, Mamma—Mr Washbourne?"

Lady Falconer groaned in despair. " 'Tis no matter to waste precious time over, child, only please *do* make haste. The gentleman has consumed three dishes of India tea already and seems reluctant to partake of a fourth. Besides, your father is eating us right out of simnel cake."

With that her ladyship fussed away to dance attendance upon her honoured guest whilst Sharonne did as she was bid, her head and heart in a state of desolation about this Mr Washbourne whom, it seemed abundantly evident, was yet another prospective son-in-law that her mother had inveigled to the house on the pretext of taking tea. As can well be appreciated, Sharonne was in no state of being at this crucial time to give due consideration to another choice of husband when she yet cherished fond hopes of hearing from the first. Therefore, it was with heavy heart and tread that she descended to the parlour anon, her shapeliness adorned in the apple-green muslin worn over moderate hoops and caught up round the hem by dark green velvet ribbons which also confined her auburn curls in an attractive top-knot, apart from one or two wayward tendrils which caressed her cheek. Cream triple lace flounces trimmed the elbow-length sleeves while the neck was styled fashionably, if revealingly, low. Yes, the gown certainly wrought a transformation in her appearance, but, alas, could do little to transform her dejected spirits.

Pausing outside the parlour door, she inhaled a few deep breaths to compose her countenance, firmly decided upon discouraging this Mr Washbourne most emphatically—offensively, if need be—and with eyes demurely downcast, she entered the room.

"La, there you are at last, Sharonne, my dove!" cried her mother, a full octave above her normal pitch as she gushed forward, all flapping fingers and fixed smiles. "I do declare we were quite despairing of you, were we not, husband?"

"Indeed, Agatha," concurred the blustering voice of Sir Giles. "Humph, come ye in, child, and make y'r curtsy to Mr Washbourne here!"

Out of her side-eye Sharonne saw the gentleman rise to his feet—very elegant feet—upon her left, and whilst her mamma clucked and her papa 'humphed' she went through the mechanical motion of formal greeting decreed by convention—decorous curtsy, eyes upon his gold buckled shoes, whilst proffering her ice-cold hand for him to do with whate'er he felt inclined.

A rustle of turquoise-blue brocade, the touch of his warm strong fingers, then the well-modulated sound of his voice.

"Your devoted servant, Miss Falconer. I am honoured to be thus able to further our acquaintance."

That voice! Her eyes leapt to his, to stare in speechless amazement.

"Edmund!" she gasped finally, which seemed to be all she was capable of articulating as she fought an overwhelming urge to fling herself into his arms—decidedly not the formal procedure laid down by propriety.

This her mother apparently sensed, for she hurriedly placed a restraining hand upon her daughter's arm.

"Do not you recall Mr Washbourne, Sharonne dear? He vows most adamantly that he made your acquaintance at Northumberland House."

"Permit me to stress, ma'am," Mr Washbourne addressed his hostess with urbanity, "that your delightful daughter was attended by so many gallant swains I cannot, and indeed do not, expect her to even recall my name."

"Oh, yes! Yes! O-Of course I do," breathed Sharonne, her shining eyes not once deflecting from his blue. "H-How could I possibly forget Mr W-Washbourne."

It was Edmund! Her Edmund! He had invented the name of Washbourne, for how could he expect to be welcomed into the home of her family under his legitimate one? Her dreams had eventually come true, he was here! He had come to claim her hand and carry her off to his castle like her knight in armour!

Sharonne could vaguely hear her father saying something about Mr Washbourne soliciting his permission to formally address her, and retiring discreetly from the room with her mother. No sooner were the two alone than the Marquess took her in his arms and kissed her once lightly on the lips, again more ardently, then stood back to appraise her.

"I apologise most profusely for the inordinate delay, dear one," he stated, his eyes traveling her length and breadth. "I'm afraid my brother's affairs took a deal longer to attend to than I anticipated. I presume you are of the same heart and mind as when we met?"

"Oh, Edmund, how can you doubt it? My faith and love have never wavered for a single moment, I knew you would come some day!" She deviated slightly from the truth in her effort to reassure him, wishing he would seize her to him and kiss her again—and, unable to restrain herself, took the initiative and threw herself into his arms as she had felt the urge to do earlier.

"Oh, Edmund, I love you!" she gasped fervently. "I never dreamed I could ever love anyone as much as I love you! I can't eat, sleep—or sometimes even breathe!" She gave a nervous little giggle. "If you hadn't come today I'd have pined to death by the end of the week, I swear."

Again he kissed her, and smiled as he put her from him, a forced smile, as if something troubled him.

"Sharonne," he ventured cautiously, and she waited agog, hanging upon his lips for the ardent declaration of love she felt was her due, but his mind was diverting along another road. "I trust you understand that my reprieve is merely temporary?"

"Reprieve? From what, Edmund?" she questioned, glancing up into his serious face, stressed to advantage by the impeccable white Venetian lace beneath his bearded chin.

"Reprieve from revealing my true identity, which I must do ere the night is out."

"Oh, no! Not yet, Edmund—I beg you!"

"Sharonne, I have no choice. It is wrong to deceive your parents thus, apart from which, your father will be anxious to draw up the Marriage Contract and—"

"Yes, yes! I understand, Edmund—but, please, j-just give me a little while to break the news to them as gently as possible. Please, I beseech you to leave the confession to me, for it is absolutely vital that the moment be opportune."

It was naturally assumed by his host and hostess that Mr Washbourne—or dear Edmund, as the occasion now seemed to warrant—would not only deign to stay for supper but several days' sojourn in order that they should all become better acquainted before the marriage.

One might think it not a little irregular that Sir Giles and his good lady should be prepared to accept this Mr Washbourne so readily into their midst as a suitable husband for their beloved daughter. However, as convention—and necessity—decreed wealth and position the two most important assets in a prospective husband, and Mr Washbourne gave more than abundant evidence of these impressive qualities, denoted in his air of supreme confidence as if accustomed to delegating orders, and his fashionable apparel—which Lady Falconer swore could boast its origin from the the other side of the Channel and had obviously been smuggled into the country at considerable expense—not to mention the amethyst ring upon his right hand and the maching pin in his lace cravat, indeed, a gem the size of a pigeon's egg and surely worth a king's ransom, he was therefore privileged to merit the Falconers' implicit trust, on sight. Moreover, anyone who could name the Northumberlands amongst their intimates was welcome to anything Sir Giles and his lady wife had to offer— even their daughter!

The Falconers' cook was to be highly commended for the quantity and exceptional quality of the dishes placed before the honoured guest at such short notice. These included a glazed turkey, venison pasty, hare stuffed with herbs and cinnamon, fricassee of eggs, followed by creamed apples, whim-wham, angel cakes, almond biscuits and sweetmeats, and the whole launched upon a copious flow of home-made gooseberry wine.

Throughout the meal Sharonne battled valiantly to rally the essential courage to make the staggering revelation which would shatter the amicability betwixt her parents and the man she loved, and probably put an abrupt end to all thought of welcoming him into the family as the long-desired son-in-law. Consequently, despite the delectable array of dishes, she sat toying with her food, listening with half an ear to her mother and father's animated small-talk. Worst of all, she could feel Edmund's eye upon her the while, waiting, wondering how many more opportune moments she was going to let slip by unheeded and whether he ought not, after all, to take the initiative in her stead, for she could well appreciate his predicament. Indeed, his position was growing increasingly precarious, for with each glass of Aunt Matilda's potent wine her father imbibed his questions were becoming more and more pertinent, and Edmund's inventive genius was being stretched to incredible limits.

It was during the third course that the crisis came, and even then it was not Sharonne but Sir Giles himself who indirectly forced the issue, by probing—none too tactfully—into the source of his future son-in-law's extraordinary wealth.

"So, y're a land-owner, eh, like m'self?" declared Sir Giles with relish. "Command a tolerable few acres here, y' know. Humph! Must be every inch of three thousand."

Common courtesy ordained that Lord Ashton appear

agreeably impressed, though he discreetly declined a comment.

"Well, Mr Washbourne? And what might the grand total o' your acres amount to, eh?" pursued his host—to Sharonne's acute disconcertion. "I presume ye have counted 'em? Ha! Ha!"

He obviously thought the jest worth a guffaw or two, but he guffawed alone—though her ladyship was heard to emit an affected chuckle—for Sharonne and Edmund were some three jumps ahead, already anticipating the consequences of the latter's answer.

"I command something in the region of forty-eight, sir," his lordship spoke up anon, with the utmost condescension.

Sir Giles blew out his ruddy cheeks and up shot his bushy brows.

"Thunder an' turf! Forty-eight acres and ye have the effrontery to call y'self a land-owner?"

"Not forty-eight acres, Sir Giles—forty-eight thousand."

An excruciating silence fell all around as everyone held their breath, except Sir Giles himself who seemed to have stopped breathing altogether.

"F-Forty-eight *thousand*!" ejaculated he at last, eyeballs protruding like doorknobs. "Damn ye, sir! D'ye seek to mock me? I know of no one outside o' the aristocracy who ever owned half as much!"

Again the Marquess looked to Sharonne to fulfil her promise, but in vain for she was struck dumb with apprehension and extremely loath to betray her dearest Edmund now that she could plainly see which way the wind of change was blowing. Thus she sat torn between the two men she loved most in the world, glancing in desperation at each in turn, unable to remain loyal to one without betraying the other. Meanwhile, Lady Falconer's eye shuttled back and forth also, as she sat mumchance wondering what all the dissension was about, for she had quite lost the gist of the conversation three topics ago and was concerned only for her husband's state of health which had been rather delicate since the seizure he had suffered on the occasion of his son's tragic death. To work himself into such a taking could have disastrous consequences, and when all was said and done, was it not supposed to be a *happy* gathering?

"Well, sirrah?" prompted Sir Giles eventually, "Are ye an aristocrat? Or a confounded liar?"

"Father!" exclaimed Sharonne, aghast.

"Giles!" protested his wife simultaneously, for to call one's guest such a thing was a shocking breach of etiquette—even if the term were justified.

But Mr Washbourne was no ordinary guest. He was at the Falconers' home to claim Sharonne's hand and so had to acquit himself honourably 'neath her father's scrutiny, in which case truths needed to be aired.

Sharonne winced and closed her eyes tightly at the harsh grinding noise of Edmund's chair as he pushed it back upon the polished floor to rise slowly to his feet and draw himself up to his full height, dwarfing them all with his tall arrogant figure as he gazed contemptuously down, every inch of him proclaiming aloud his birth, before he orally confirmed it.

"I am an aristocrat," he returned curtly, "of whose name you might not approve."

"Why, sir? What is your name if 'tis not Washbourne?" demanded Sir Giles angrily.

116

His lordship cast a final glance at Sharonne as he paused, granting her this last opportunity to realise her earnest desire, yet of which she seemed reluctant to avail herself as she sat with head downbent, unable to meet his challenging look, and so he went on to disrupt the tense silence.

"My name is St Claire—Edmund St Claire, Marquess of Ashton."

Lady Falconer unleashed an inarticulate cry and began to tremble from head to foot in a kind of nervous spasm, while her husband fell back in his chair, his eyes starting from his head at the man before him, unable to credit his barefaced audacity in coming thus to his house, dining 'neath his roof, and calmly requesting the hand of his daughter—Jonathan's sister! Jonathan! The son he had loved more than life itself, who had been cut ruthlessly down by, ostensibly, this Marquess of Ashton!

Sir Giles's next move was to rise afoot on a par with his guest—though he fell ten inches short of his height —his face murderous and drawn as he glared malevolently across the depleted dishes, but before he could utter a syllable Sharonne interceded.

"No, Father! Wait! I beg you will not act in haste! You are terribly mistaken!" she cried out in anguish, reaching out to stay him. "Edmund is innocent of Jonathan's blood! It was not he but his brother, the fourth Marquess, who—"

"I don't care if it was his great-grandsire!" thundered Sir Giles, pounding the table to the clatter and tinkle of glass and china, as her ladyship dissolved in tears and fled the scene with her shaking hands clutched to her throbbing temples. "Sirrah!" went on her husband, verbally attacking the Marquess—primarily because he had no weapon to hand with which to attack him physically. "You will quit my house this instant! And you will never see my daughter again—"

"No! No, Father!" screamed Sharonne in horror, running to Edmund's arms in open contravention of her parent's command. "I love him! He is blameless—utterly blameless! And I am determined to wed him!"

"He is a St Claire!" Sir Giles rounded savagely on his daughter. "His family butchered your brother! Sir, you will unhand my daughter and get out of my house at once before I have you thrown out and horsewhipped for your impudence!"

"Father, you wouldn't dare!" cried Sharonne defiantly, positioning herself protectively in front of the man she loved, her arms outflung. "If he goes, then I shall go too."

"You will do no such thing!" bellowed her father, turning purple with rage. "You will follow your mother abovestairs, you insolent jade, and remain in your bedchamber petitioning heaven for absolution of your dire sin until I give you permission to show yourself again!"

"You forget, Sir Giles," sounded the calm voice of the Marquess. "Your daughter has long attained her majority and is therefore lawfully permitted to make her own decisions."

Admittedly Sir Giles had overlooked this vital point and was certainly not endeared to his enemy for the poignant reminder as he returned a baleful frown.

"Devil take ye, sir!" he rasped furiously. "If put to the test do you think she would choose you in preference to her own kith and kin? Her own flesh and blood? Do you honestly believe that any daughter of mine

118

would willingly elect to go through life bearing the name of her brother's murderer?"

"As you evidently think otherwise, why not ask her?" parried my lord with equanimity. "You have nought to lose."

The older man weighed this subtle move, very much of the opinion that no matter what age females were they were seldom capable of deciding anything for themselves other than how to burst the sides of their dressing closets with more fripperies and fal-lals than they would have time to wear if they lived to see ninety-nine. But Sharonne was rather different, he was proud to admit. True, she was high spirited, but nonetheless gifted with common-sense and had been reared in a decent God-fearing house, therefore was well able to detect right from wrong.

"As you will," he growled, confident of his daughter's decision now that the issue had reached this crucial climax and she was to be confronted with making a final choice between her own mother and father and this shallow rake, this ne'er-do-well with whom she imagined herself to be in love. Love? Ha! The fellow had never loved anyone in his entire life half so much as himself—a typical example of the exquisites of the day! No, granted the option, he was quite certain which his daughter would choose.

"Well, Sharonne?" he snapped, smarting 'neath this humiliation and already planning some commensurate penance for her to atone for this merry dance she was creating when it was all over. "Make your decision, girl, and let's ha' done with this absurd farce! Do you stay with the mother and father who have raised you, fed and clothed you, given you all your heart desired, and loved you more constantly than this reprobate will in future?"

Sharonne's terrible agony of soul was manifest in her sweet face as she prevaricated between the two, ultimately forced into making the decision she had inwardly dreaded, yet which had hung relentlessly over her head like the Sword of Damocles ever since she discovered that Edmund was a St Claire. It was not that the decision itself was so very difficult, for she was already firmly decided upon her course. No, it was the pain and heartache she must bring to the one she must deny and the words she ought to select to soften the blow.

With hesitant steps she approached her parent, trying desperately to quell the anguish rising within her and the tears pricking her eyes.

"F-Father," she faltered in a tremulous voice. "I—I must go with E-Edmund . . . I—I'm sorry, b-but I must. . . . I h-hope you will under . . . stand. . . ."

Sir Giles Falconer stood petrified in disbelief as her words fought to register in his bewildered brain, until their full import struck him with dynamic force. And as Sharonne bent forward to kiss him fondly he pushed her roughly away and swung round on his heel, his back to her.

"Then go!" he rasped hoarsely over his shoulder. "Go, and don't ever return! I shall break the news to your mother—now go quickly!"

And when next he looked, his daughter and the visitor were gone.

120

4

THE light equipage emblazoned with the Ashton coat-of-arms and drawn by a team of six, tore through the night along the St Albans road as if the entire underworld were on its rear axle, stopping only for the briefest refreshment and a change of horses at every third posting house to be off again into the pitch darkness. At Watford, the Marquess himself climbed on to the box to snatch the ribbons from his coachman with a curse of impatience and set off as if Lucifer were indeed in command, whipping the cattle into a foaming lather in his determination to extract every ounce of energy out of them—whilst the local peasantry hastily crossed themselves as the coach flew by, deeming little to choose betwixt the two arch-fiends.

Meanwhile, Sharonne lay curled up on the red velvet seat doing her level best to remain thereon and secure some sleep despite the violent motion, whilst wondering why her noble lord was in such tempestuous haste to get her to his country home when he had kept her languishing several months awaiting his call.

It was almost noon next day when Sharonne got her first impressive glimpse of Court St Claire—surprised, though she knew not why, to find it of Tudor origin, with the characteristic dark oak beams of its half-timberwork contrasting strikingly with the whitewashed plasterwork as it rambled along the horizon in typical old-world charm, whilst landscaped grounds stretched away on either side of the two-mile driveway as far as the eye could see.

The coach finally swept to a standstill at the main entrance and as a flunkey ran from the house to let down the coach steps the Marquess descended from the box and assisted Sharonne to alight, then escorted her up the three shallow stairs into his home.

As the interior was found to compliment the exterior in every facet, Sharonne was not to be disappointed with the mass of oak panelling, ponderous oak staircase mounted with rampant lions, elaborately carved vaulted ceilings, and mullioned windows set high in the walls. However, as to be expected, the Great Hall was the most awe-inspiring room in the house with its hammer-beam ceiling, and walls covered with every conceivable weapon known to man from crossbows and broadswords to rapiers and flintlocks, some of which were small enough to hold in the palm of one's hand, while suits of armour wielding shields and battle-axes occupied the four corners, and two huge gaping stone fireplaces confronted each other in the centres of the two longer walls. Despite the deficiency of windows, the Hall was ablaze with light from six wrought-iron chandeliers suspended overhead, and torchères and candelabra scattered at random.

Nevertheless, although the day was typically warm for the month of August, Sharonne felt suddenly chilled and shivered involuntarily as she clung the tighter to Edmund's arm. Icy fingers seemed to grip her heart as if she could sense another presence, the presence of Gabriel St Claire, of his bygone spirit which felt to be all around—or perhaps it was not quite as bygone as she wished to think, and was there, unseen. . . .

"Alas, the old house has been uninhabited for some considerable while, I'm afraid, it will need time to readjust to having us 'neath its roof," the Marquess apprised her on a note of concern, though Sharonne got a vague impression that his concern was more on the house's behalf than her own as his eyes lingered affectionately upon each item as if he were transported back to another world, maybe the far distant world of his childhood—when he suddenly drew himself up. "But come, Miss Falconer—"

'Miss Falconer?' She inwardly queried the formality.

"—you must be somewhat tired after such a harrowing journey. A chamber is already available; I shall have you conducted hence at once where you may rest awhile. A tray will be sent up to you directly."

The minimal flicker of an eyebrow and a footman was at his side bowing low to receive his instructions, and looking uncommonly like the footman who had rushed out to let down the steps of the coach. In fact, Sharonne got the distinct impression that in spite of my lord's extravagant wealth the entire house was in the hands of no more than half a dozen servants.

"I trust the room will be to your satisfaction," he continued addressing her, "though 'tis merely temporary. A bridal chamber has been specially prepared to which you will be admitted later tonight—after the ceremony."

Sharonne's eyes shot wide in surprise. "Tonight? W-We are to be m-married, tonight?"

"At midnight. It is all arranged—unless you would prefer to lodge at some questionable hostelry in the local village until you consider the moment more conducive?"

"N-No, my lord—er—tonight will be conducive enough," she hastened to assure him. "I-It's just that it is r-rather sudden and I am quite unprepared. Indeed," she forced a weak laugh. "I was not given time to gather my gowns together before we left."

"I'm sure you will find everything you need in your chamber. If this is not so, I trust you will not hesitate to inform me," he returned, the quintessence of courtesy as he swept her a leg, about to retire when he paused on afterthought. "Select any gown you wish for the occasion. It matters little which you choose as it will not be seen by anyone of consequence, other than myself."

"Why, will not there be any guests?"

"No, only the two essential witnesses, the rôles of which my valet and your personal maid will fulfil."

"No guests!" she exclaimed with incredulity.

"No, Miss Falconer!" he stressed with strained forbearance. "Under the circumstances I should consider any kind of formal celebration distasteful in the extreme, and am rather surprised to find you so grossly out of sympathy with me."

On the contrary his bride was entirely in sympathy with him in not desiring a great show of ostentation with hundreds of curious though distinguished guests milling around them, and should have been exceedingly loath to have been obliged to suffer such following her tragic parting from her beloved parents the previous day. It was just that it was all a little unusual.

Howbeit, if Sharonne intended proffering an apology in any shape or form for the misunderstanding, alas, she was granted no opportunity, for my lord gave a curt bow and strode off to the left, leaving the lackey to undertake the task of escorting his future wife abovestairs.

124

Yes, the room was certainly comfortable and tastefully furnished in blue and cream damask, but most comfortable of all to Sharonne at that moment, perhaps, was the huge fourposter bed holding full sway in the centre and upon which she lost no time in settling herself. And despite all the trials and tribulations besetting her she was soon enveloped in the arms of Morpheus. Of course, following such a racking journey this might well be appreciated, also, that she managed to sleep quite soundly until ten o'clock when she was gently wakened by a somewhat apprehensive girl, a little better attired than the regular chambermaid and judged to be about two years younger than Sharonne herself, and who bore the requisitioned tray—a cold collation with ratafia—to fortify her mistress for the impending marriage.

Sharonne then ascertained that the girl's name was Mary—her new personal maid who had come to help her prepare for the ceremony. Having little appetite, Sharonne rejected the food but partook of the cordial, hoping it might steady her nerves for what was to come.

Sure enough as predicted, the Marquess had furnished her with several gowns of varying hues and materials, hoop-petticoats, shifts, riding habits—indeed, everything she could possibly require for the time being in her new home, as she discovered upon venturing into the dressing closet. Furthermore she found cosmetics, perfumes, and jewels in abundance, and accessories of every description, including satin slippers, silk stockings, fans, fripperies and gloves, and, what was more, of the correct size and shape behind which she detected a keen power of observation.

Her choice of gown for the ceremony was not difficult to decide, for there was but one white gown in the collection, which was an open robe of satin brocade with long train and the petticoat and stomacher decorated with tiny pearls. Obviously it was the gown my lord intended she should wear, for upon the dresser lay a casket in which was bedded a beautiful pearl tiara—in truth, a perfect match.

This extreme generosity on the Marquess's part helped in some measure to atone to Sharonne for his rather abrupt manner earlier and she was now prepared to overlook the incident, particularly as it was to be their wedding day, and he had, after all, driven long and hard and was probably even more fatigued than she had been.

The maid Mary seemed to be expert enough at her tasks, though almost as nervous as she as she deftly arranged her mistress's luxurious auburn curls in a style so appealing in its simplicity as to create a most astounding effect. However, the toilet throughout was blanketed in disconcerting quiet, almost as if the girl had been expressly forbidden by the Marquess to address her mistress or respond to her enquiries, and was terrified to gainsay him.

At fifteen minutes to midnight Sharonne stood poised before her mirror—surely the most radiant of brides, with a myriad candles flickering all around, glinting and flashing upon the pearls and silver adorning her nuptial regalia, but nevertheless creating a strange illusion, an uncanny illusion, with the vivid contrasting darkness beyond as if she were not really there at all, but part of another world, a world of ghostly figures, spectres and . . . Gabriel St Claires. The illusion gradually grew stronger and stronger until it became so real she could actually see that pale, evil yet angelically handsome face mocking her from behind her reflection, the brilliant sheen of his long fair hair gleaming in the ethereal candlelight as he flung back his head with that proud insolence peculiar to him and laughed. No, not his habitual inane laugh, but a hearty laugh, as if he were enjoying some huge jest at her expense. She could see him quite distinctly and hear the sound of his cruel contemptuous laughter resounding in her ears, and she clapped her hands over them, closing her eyes tightly to shut out sight and sound of him while shouting, screaming, for the gruesome vision to go away and leave her in peace—when she felt a touch on her arm and she looked up to see Edmund by her side, resplendent in cream brocade sprigged with gold, his face and hair enhanced by a cascade of white Flanders lace beneath his chin, while a sprinkling of diamonds completed the effect.

"Sharonne, what ails you, child?" he besought her, his brow creased in concern. "Is something not to your satisfaction?"

The unexpected sight of her future husband banished the horrifying image instantly, and like a small child she threw herself into his arms to be comforted, for it had left her feeling a trifle shaken.

"Is it Gabriel?" he murmured briefly as he held her close.

"Y-Yes . . . I s-saw him . . . qu-quite vividly. . . ."

The Marquess dismissed the maid with a nod as he drew his bride deeper into his arms to comfort her.

"Oh, Edmund!" she breathed anxiously, clinging to him in fear of the unknown. "D-Do you sometimes feel that he is n-not truly d-dead . . . but is actually alive

127

s-some . . . where . . . watching us . . . everything w-we do?"

"No, Sharonne," he answered untruthfully, for how could he speak what was in his heart and risk alarming her even more, and upon this of all nights?

As Edmund had not fallen victim to these alarming visions and did not sense his brother's presence, then Sharonne reasoned they had to be a figment of her own guilty conscience, due to the terrible burden she bore. Consequently, there was only one thing to do—confess everything to Edmund now, this very night, and then they would never disturb her again . . . would they?

"Edmund, there is something I must divulge about your brother, something truly dreadful! I-It burdens my heart and unless I confess it now, this very moment, I fear our m-marriage will not b-be l-lawful!"

He released her and in a gesture of impatience flung away to the windows.

"If it concerns Gabriel I've no wish to hear it! To-night of all nights, Sharonne, I will not have him coming between us!"

"V-Very well, E-Edmund," she faltered, loath to anger him when all was supposed to be revelry and joy, doing her utmost to regain her self-control.

"Have you recovered your composure?" he turned to query.

"Y-Yes, Edmund."

"Good! Then come, let me see if you do justice to my fastidious taste."

Sharonne positioned herself three paces in front of him, apprehensively gnawing her lip as he meandered round her, viewing her from every angle in an awesome silence.

128

"Yes," he conceded at length to her unalloyed joy, banishing Gabriel's visitation completely. "I must confess the effect is quite astounding, Sharonne, you look soul-stirringly beautiful. . . ."

This was no overstatement. Indeed, Sharonne looked everything a bride ought and more, her becoming face glowing with an inner radiance, yet her wide hazel eyes nurturing an element of doubt in their depths, the devastating effect furthered by the overall aura of innocence which the maid had taken such pains to preserve in the caress of her soft golden hair upon her naked shoulders, the minimum of colouring to her lips and cheeks, and the simple pearl necklace clasped about her ivory throat. Had she but known it, it was this very innocence which was her most vital link to the Marquess's heart and her whole future happiness.

It was an unconscionable while that Lord Ashton stood regarding his bride, drinking in the intoxicating sight of her, savouring every single moment as if he expected to be suddenly stricken blind on the morrow and should never again be privileged to gaze thus upon her —so long, in fact, that Sharonne flushed deeply with embarrassment, yet profound pleasure that he should be so acutely affected. But still he did not avert his eyes as he ventured slowly forward and took her revently in his arms to kiss her long and tenderly as he had never kissed her before. No ordinary kiss, but a kiss of infinite beauty, almost sacred, as if she were an immaculate goddess and he was half-afraid to touch her lest he fall helplessly beneath her spell, like Ulysses and the Sirens.

At length my lord led his bride from the room, through a series of chambers, the Small Gallery bedecked with miniatures, and the Long Gallery boasting a fine collection of portraits, bronzes and porcelain, and on to the stairs which they descended in silence and on through the Great Hall. At the farther end they passed through a stone Gothic archway and into another chamber with tapestry-covered walls. Here the Marquess paused to light a lanthorn, proclaiming the fact that they were about to venture into darkness. Again he took her hand and guided her through a narrow passage, down a flight of spiralling stone steps and out into an open courtyard. As they traversed this, the dim outline of a building loomed into view, built of stone, and passing through another door Sharonne found herself inside a small anteroom, lit by two candles, with yet another door at the opposite side.

My lord released her to advance to this other door and peer out, then he returned and put down the lanthorn, his high heels ringing out on the stone floor. The interior of the strange building was somewhat musty and chill and Sharonne shivered, not so much with the cold as the eerie atmosphere coupled with the sudden poignant appreciation of the crucial step she was about to take without the support or blessing of her dear parents. A tear of self-pity trickled down her nose and splashed on to her hand, and she sniffed.

"Sharonne?" came my lord's voice from the shadows. "You aren't weeping?"

"N-No," she squeaked in an attempted whisper.

A glass was promptly pushed into her hands and she was told to drink. Her tears soon subsided as the spirit tingled in her veins and she proffered an apology for being so childishly silly.

"W-Where are we, Edmund?"

"We are in the vestry of my private chapel. Are you ready?"

"Yes, Edmund."

Implanting a bouquet of roses in her arms and a kiss upon her forehead, the Marquess led her through the last door and into the chapel. This was even darker than the vestry with all the candlelight concentrated upon the altar at the farther end. Due to the deathly silence, the sound of their heels upon the stone seemed magnified a thousandfold as they proceeded down the aisle gradually merging from the darkness into the gruesome flickering shadows and finally the bright light of the candelabra adorning the altar.

As they neared the bottom Sharonne started, as a cleric mysteriously appeared and commenced the extraordinary ceremony without delay, and jumped as his sing-song voice rang out, resounding round the dank austere walls, though she really did not see much purpose in addressing a congregation when there was obviously no congregation to address. While his voice droned on she strained her eyes in the darkness to determine if the church were in fact as deserted as it seemed to be, but she could see very little apart from the first three rows of pews.

All at once it did not appear to be a wedding ceremony at all, but instead, some kind of satanic rite with the cold weird feeling, the peculiar aroma—probably incense—and the high priest himself with his hands held aloft, standing silhouetted in the candlelight like some huge black bird of prey hovering, ready to devour them at any moment.

As the strange ritual got under way Sharonne emitted

a gasp as two apparitions slowly emerged from the darkened chapel to take up position on either side of herself and the Marquess, though it should not have surprised her to any marked degree if they had stepped out of the very walls! Evidently they were the witnesses, and upon closer inspection she did indeed discover them to be his lordship's valet, and Mary, her personal maid.

But contrary to the supposition of both my Lord Marquess and his bride, the two menials were by no means the only witnesses at the macabre ceremony, for behind one of the twelve Gothic stone pillars there skulked one of dubious intent, clad in black freize double-caped surtout, the top collar buttoned high about his ears—not merely to protect his face from the cold but to protect it from identification—a person seemingly lacking respect for his hallowed environment judging by the way he tugged his cocked hat still further over his eyes, ruthless eyes which absorbed every detail of the drama being enacted before him. Indeed, although the stranger lacked respect for this House of God, he in no wise lacked interest in the ritual itself, for he had gone to exceedingly great lengths and inconvenience in order to be present, and should not have risked missing it for a king's ransom! In fact, so agitated did he become when the cleric cried aloud for 'any man to show any just cause why the couple might not lawfully be joined together' he almost betrayed himself completely by taking an eager pace forward from behind his pillar—to back hastily into the shadows again on afterthought, trusting no sound had been heard.

No, apparently something had occurred to him prompting him to wait a more propitious moment, and he pulled his collar up even higher so that nought but his eyes, two pinpoints of gleaming malevolence, were visible beneath the brim of his beaver hat.

The ceremony was not a long one, and just then the priest pronounced the benediction on the happy pair and promptly disappeared, leaving the bridegroom to lead his bride from the altar down the aisle with nought but the sound of their footsteps and breathing for accompaniment. Even the witnesses had seemingly immersed back into the walls. All, in fact, except the uninvited guest still hovering furtively behind the pillar, waiting, watching, as the couple quitted the church to return to the house, his malicious eye riveted upon them until the door closed and they could be seen no more, when he gave licence to a low rumbling laugh graduating to a blood-curdling cackle which echoed ghoulishly round the sinister empty interior as if it erupted from the very depths of hell.

But just as suddenly he regained his self-control, and snarled into his caped surtout:

"Aye, my Lord Marquess! Enjoy her whilst ye may . . ."—before he too vanished out into the night.

5

ALTHOUGH an elaborate wedding breakfast was spread
before the Marquess and his bride, they did nothing
more than pick at one or two irresistible delicacies.
Oddly enough, though this minimal amount was consumed the meal itself seemed to last an interminable
length of time, and when extreme weariness finally
overcame Sharonne, prompting her to rise from the
table, craving her lord's indulgence that she be allowed
to retire, she found it stranger still that he should seek
to actually detain her when according to custom and
the dictates of Mother Nature he ought to have abetted
her suggestion with frenzied enthusiasm.

But instead, she was to discover yet another facet to
the Marquess's nature, for again his humour had
changed. She was pleased to note that he was more
amiable, but commented little, being more inclined to
listen to her animated chatter, and whenever he elected
to do so it was with the utmost courtesy, a smile and the
occasional kiss upon her dainty fingers.

No, it was nothing in his lordship's manner or what
he said which occurred to Sharonne as unusual but
more in the way she found him oft-times regarding her
in variable expressions—amusement, admiration, curiosity, and profound pathos. Even a peculiar blend of
confusion and desire, when passion would flare so intensely in his eyes she was forced for modesty's sake to
screen her blushing countenance.

Love and longing, coupled with a degree of apprehension, danced a lively rigadoon in Sharonne's heart when her maid eventually entered at two o'clock to escort her to the bridal chamber, but she was again assailed with the strange feeling at my lord's obvious reluctance to let her go, though nevertheless, permission was granted.

However, all qualms were momentarily banished from her heart when she entered the bridal chamber and gasped in awe at the wonder which met her gaze. Roses of every hue were arranged in profusion around the room, while white gauze curtains trimmed with pink satin knots graced the oriel windows and the most vital thing of all, the bed, which commanded immediate attention amidst the rose arbour, tall and imposing, draped entirely in white and pink with coverlets and pillows in matching satin. White bearskin rugs covered the spacious floor while on the brocade stool by the dresser lay a night-shift of diaphanous white silk, sprigged with pink.

It was now that Sharonne appreciated further advantages of a quiet marriage for under the rules of custom she would have been obliged to suffer the humiliation of fatuous rituals such as 'untying the garter' and 'flinging the stocking' which she could not have borne.

Again Mary worked quickly and silently in preparing her new mistress for the nuptial bed, adorning her shapeliness in the diaphanous shift and combing out her long rich golden hair, finally adding a sprinkling of delicately scented flower water to complement the surroundings. Last of all, Sharonne climbed into the great four-poster whilst Mary withdrew to inform the Marquess that his Marchioness awaited his pleasure.

The Marchioness was destined to have a long wait, a

very long wait. For the first full hour she lay rigid with anticipation, which gradually waned to impatience, pique, disappointment, and finally utter despair. And shortly before the grey dawn began to penetrate the flimsy curtains, Sharonne fell off to sleep.

The sun was already long risen when she was awakened by a scratch upon the door heralding Mary with her traditional cup of hot chocolate, and of whom Sharonne lost no time in querying news of her husband whilst striving bravely to assume an airy tone, though it was painfully obvious by his undisturbed side of the bed, Sharonne's lacklustre gaze, and the total absence of all things masculine that the Marquess had not set foot near his bride throughout the entire night. However, if the girl noticed any of this she was much too well disciplined to give the slightest intimation of it as she drew back the bed-curtains and humbly informed her mistress that his lordship had gone off on horse some three hours agone and had not yet returned—uttered in a tone which implied it the most natural thing in the world for a bridegroom to do, presumably to spare Sharonne embarrassment. Even so, at the news Sharonne was overcome with a powerful inclination to cling to the comforts of the bed all day but realised that such childish reaction would serve only to draw more attention to the incongruous situation and so she ordered the girl to select her a gown and help her dress, determined that everything should appear as normal as possible. Howbeit, by the time the Marquess eventually returned—at ten minutes after seven in the evening—Sharonne was perilously near to yelling her grievance from the gabled rooftop to ease the crucifying pain in her heart at his wilful neglect.

Nevertheless, at prompt nine that evening her noble lord condescended to sup with her, at which singular honour she did not know whether to rejoice, repine, or do him bodily ill. Had she chosen to rejoice she should have done so somewhat prematurely for his conversation throughout was more stinted than during the wedding feast. Not once did my lord seek to break the painful silence. Even his greeting upon her entrance amounted to nothing more than a stiff bow and a flicker of the lips, intended to be a smile. Moreover, he had quite deliberately elected to dine *en formalité* and had positioned her where protocol demanded, at the opposite end of the twenty-foot-long refectory table, no doubt to add further discouragement to conversation. Indeed, why he had condescended to sup with her at all Sharonne could not cease wondering.

Both made admirable pretence at doing a hearty justice to all seven courses though, in truth, scarcely a single platterful was devoured between them. However, his lordship did have frequent recourse to the wine decanter, which was his only external sign of inward disturbance. His wife, conversely, became more agitated with every passing second, evident in the way she fidgeted with anything to hand, gnawed her bottom lip, and at intervals cleared her throat as if about to overture some comment but abruptly changed her mind at his forbidding glance.

Her emotional crisis reached its climax during the final course when, unable to endure the torment any longer, she leapt up and swept down the length of the table to sink at his feet in a curtsy of contrition.

"Edmund, what have I done to offend you?" she besought him, with troubled gaze. "Why are you so cold towards me?"

Her eyes raked his obdurate features for a sign of clemency but without success. In fact, the mere twitch of a facial muscle was the only indication he gave of having even heard her as he mechanically replenished his glass with burgundy.

"Tell me, I implore you, my lord, then I shall be able to crave your forgiveness, vow not to do whatever it is again, and we can be happy as we were before. Please, Edmund, what is it that has turned you away from me?"

As he still did not respond, Sharonne placed a hand upon his huge embroidered cuff and felt him instinctively stiffen, though he voiced no objection. Then panic seized her—it was Gabriel! He had discovered her secret from someone, though she knew not whom nor how, for there was no other living soul aware of it . . . except Gabriel himself!

"I-Is it Gabriel? Y-You have perhaps discovered s-something . . . concerning him and myself . . . which you d-do . . . not l-like?"

He winced.

Exactly as she suspected! This left no alternative but to confess the whole sordid deed and have done with it, trusting she and their profound love would survive the full blast of his justifiable . . . what? How would he react? Would he be angry? Indifferent? Or sick with disgust? Oh, angry! Please let him be angry, she prayed inwardly, as long as he forgave her eventually. She could never endure a lifelong punishment of his cold indifference!

"Oh, Edmund," she heaved in one great unburdening

sigh, resting her cheek on his knee. "I can almost feel glad that you finally know my terrible secret for I swear I could not have borne the burden of it much longer."

"Confess, dear wife, precisely what it is that burdens your soul," he requested with overdone urbanity. "I wouldst fain hear it from your own lips."

"I—I did something dreadful, Edmund! S-Something truly unforgivable, to atone for J-Jonathan's death—" she choked, racked with anguish, and swallowed hard to regain her composure. "I—I hired three felons to k-kidnap Gabriel . . . they plied him w-with gin . . . I cut off h-his hair . . . st-stained him with walnut j-juice . . . and . . . and—"

"Yes?"

Sharonne forced herself to continue though the recollection of the ghastly business made her stomach heave in revulsion.

"—he was s-stripped of his . . . f-fine clothes, and then I . . . I . . . oh, Edmund, I can't go on! I can't! P-Please—"

"Go on, dear wife, confess the whole," he insisted in calm, though unrelenting, tone.

"Edmund, you are cruel! Cruel!" she sobbed into the voluminous folds of his claret coat. "I—I summoned the . . . p-press gang . . . they dragged him a-away . . . I—I don't know what became of him after that, Edmund—I swear!" she cried wildly, raising her distraught eyes to his inscrutable face. "I tried to tell you before our marriage, but you stopped me! Why, Edmund? Why? Why didn't you call the bailiff to arrest and hang me? Then you would have been rid of me forever!"

"Aye, a wife is legally protected by her husband, is

she not?" he commented rather than queried, sipping the burgundy with due deliberation. "And exactly how much did you pay these three fine felons to commit your dastardly deed?"

"T-Two thousand pounds—it was as much as I could manage," she admitted forlornly. "They agreed to accept half that amount until they discovered who it was I would have them kidnap. I suppose I was fortunate to acquire their services at all, for your brother had earned a considerable reputation, and several had previously refused to have anything to do with it."

"And you do deem the money well spent? Whether Gabriel be alive or dead, do you feel your brother's death has been amply recompensed?"

An intonation in his voice struck an uncomfortable chord in Sharonne's heart, as if he were wholly impervious to her suffering, his brother's, and also Jonathan's untimely death.

"Yes," she responded, more than a little piqued. "I'd have given twice—nay, thrice that amount for Jonathan!"

"You must forgive me, my dear, but I'm afraid brotherly affection is an emotion quite alien to me," he observed on a sour note, as if resenting her the experience. "I doubt prodigiously if I'd have sacrificed two pence to ransom the carcass of mine."

Her heart suddenly went out to him, being cursed with a brother like Gabriel St Claire, and she somewhat imprudently voiced her sympathy.

"I'm sorry, Edmund. You must have suffered much unhappiness—"

"I don't want your confounded pity!" he rasped harshly, rising abruptly from the table and flinging

140

down his napkin to storm to the other side of the room where he took succour in much stronger drink, more suited to the occasion.

Sharonne's mouth fell disconsolately ajar as she rose up, following his irate figure with bewildered eyes, wondering where she had gone astray and what she had said to upset him so when she had been at such pains to be placating.

"E-Edmund—"

"The hour is late!" he cut her dead. "It is time you retired. Good night!"

Obviously there was not much to be gained by pursuing the matter in his present mood, and so Sharonne drew herself up erect, stifling her despondency beneath a cloak of disdain.

"If I am to retire, my Lord Marquess, would you be good enough to advise me which room you intend I should occupy?"

"Any room you wish! You have eighty-four from which to choose!"

"Then I shall choose the bridal chamber," she replied with asperity. "Who can tell? If you consume enough liquor before dawn you might even deign to treat me like a bride!"

Before he could make any requital Sharonne swept from the room with all the dignity she could summon, leaving the Marquess to drink himself into oblivion.

6

SUDDENLY there was a sound and Sharonne awoke with a start to listen intently in the darkness for the sound to come again, hoping desperately that it would be the sound she longed to hear, the sound of her husband's footfall. But all remained quiet—until it *did* come again, more distinctly. Yes, undoubtedly a footstep outside her door.

She bobbed up alert and swept back the bed-curtain to have her suspicions confirmed by the dim light of a candle flickering beneath the door.

"Edmund?" she cried out on impulse, and the light instantaneously disappeared, leaving her wondering if she had truly seen it at all.

At length she lay down and waited, determined to stay awake, her eye riveted to the bottom of the door lest he should return, but eventually, with a yawn, she drifted back to sleep. She had not lain long thus when she bobbed up again—yes! There was the light, and the footsteps pacing slowly to and fro just outside of the room.

"Edmund!" she cried as before, this time leaping up and running to the door to find—nothing. She groped the inky blackness, straining her eyes the while, but her hands contacted nought but the bare wainscotting.

Confused and dejected, Sharonne returned to her bed, rejecting the idea to light a candle and search the passage more thoroughly, for if Edmund was determined not to be seen all the candles in the world would not help her. Thus, she settled down beneath the coverlets a second time, trying to fathom the unpredictable humours of this strange man she had married as she focused a keen eye upon the door, but, as before, she began to slumber.

This time she slept soundly for a considerable while and when she eventually woke all was dark and still as it had been earlier with no sound of footsteps and no glimmer of light—but wait! What was that? There was a sound if she listened extra carefully, and quite close at hand—of breathing, and certainly not her own.

"E-Edmund?" she probed dubiously, her sleepy eyes trying to penetrate the darkness.

A veritable eon seemed to tick by ere he responded: "Yes?"

She judged the sound to be over by the first window —yes, the moon was emerging from behind the clouds and she would now see him silhouetted against the thin curtains.

"A-Are you still angry with me?"

"No, Sharonne."

"Do you despise m-me, Edmund?"

A sigh—or was it a groan?—seemed to reverberate through him.

"No more than I do myself."

The moon again became obscured and she could see him no longer, but she could still sense his presence in the blackness . . . some . . . where. . . .

"H-Have you forgiven me, Edmund?"

"For what?" —his voice was much nearer.

"For what I did to G-Gabriel?" she stammered anxiously, extending a trembling hand instinctively towards the sound, to start with a thrill when her fingers alighted upon the soft luxurious velvet through which she could feel the warm vibrant muscle of his arm. . . . Yes, he was very close now—upon the bed.

"I have nothing to forgive," he murmured as if preoccupied with something else.

"But if Gabriel is still alive somewhere, he will come seeking me. Edmund—I-I'm frightened."

However, his presence and the feel of the velvet were very comforting and she manoeuvred close enough to touch him with both hands, and eventually to rest her head upon his shoulder in blissful contentment which waxed to unadulterated joy when his arms slowly encircled her to hold her even nearer.

"Rest assured, Sharonne, you have nought to fear from Gabriel, now or ever. Besides, even if he were to return, I doubt vastly if he'd be the same Gabriel St Claire we both knew."

Once again the moon's gentle beams filtered into the room as Sharonne raised her head to gaze up into his eyes, trying to define his mood. Never had she looked more breathtakingly beautiful as the moonlight caught her head, transforming her glorious hair into molten gold as it rippled down past her white translucent shoulders where they protruded from her disordered shift, and on to rest in soft curls upon the tempting rise and fall of her matured bosom, her eyes glowing with love and adoration for the man before her, and that sweet, sweet innocence, so devastating in its simplicity which undermined his self-discipline to a precarious degree . . . while upon her inviting parted lips hovered the unspoken promises her eyes conveyed. . . .

But suddenly his were were glowing, too, two smouldering embers burning into her own. Smouldering, to burst all at once into blazing desire as he gripped her tighter, tighter, whilst his lips sought hers to scarce touch them at first, a light breath, caress, gradually increasing in pressure until he was devouring her in an explosion of wild uncontrollable passion!

Sharonne had never experienced anything like it, even during their rendezvous in the gardens of Northumberland House, and certainly not since their arrival at Court St Claire for he had hardly kissed her at all. Indeed, she had never known such a furious outburst of emotion and was surprised—and not a little shocked—to find herself responding to it with a fervour almost equal to his own.

Unexpectedly he released her to discard his coat, flinging it across the room as if it contaminated him, then seize her to him again, the sensuous feel of her warm pulsating flesh through the thin shift firing his blood still further in this closer proximity. His silver embroidered waistcoat was next to follow the coat, bringing her voluptuous body even closer.

Drugged with his intense ardour, Sharonne wallowed in rapture, yielding eagerly to the demand of his lips, his hands, his love, sinking deeper, deeper 'neath his intoxication when her heart gave a leap of ecstasy to find him prone on the bed alongside her and his demands increasing, his passion growing still more torrid, breathing into her being a new awareness of her own body, a new life, pervading her with desires she had never experienced before! Wild desires! Soul-torturing desires! A frantic desperate yearning for she knew not what— though he seemed to know well enough as he played upon her most vulnerable weaknesses with uncanny accuracy, sending thrills spiralling from the depths of her soul, whirling her to the frenzied heights of erotic bliss.

And with her entire being crying out for him to administer the antidote to this raging desire, Sharonne lay back in his arms, about to surrender herself to the ultimate sacrifice—when the whole euphoria was shattered by a mighty thundering at the main door.

The Marquess stopped dead, elevating his head to listen, wondering along with Sharonne if he had heard aright, for despite the volume of sound it seemed somewhat incredible that anyone should be paying calls at four in the morning. But it came again, louder still, and the stumbling feet of the sleepy-eyed footman were then to be heard hastening to investigate whom the noisy intruder might be.

My lord lay tensed by Sharonne, his ear cocked to catch the sound of bolts being drawn, and the door opening to admit someone—masculine, if the sonorous voice and heavy footfall on the wooden floor below-stairs were aught to go by. Lord Ashton lingered no longer, but sprang off the bed with a round curse, wrenched open the door, and strode off in the direction of the stairs to deal with the situation in no uncertain manner, leaving Sharonne emotionally suspended from the canopy of carved cupids over the nuptial bed.

For some time her spirit continued to drift in the upper hemisphere, longing ardently for her lord to return and resume the lesson—until the sound of the two men's voices raised in violent discord brought her crashing down to earth! With every sense instantly alerted Sharonne lay, her ears pricked, trying to interpret the indistinguishable rigmarole into words when the voices fell quiet to a low murmur, to rise again to such a turbulent degree that she grew alarmed and leapt out of bed. Hastily seeking her robe of white velvet trimmed with swansdown to cover her semi-nakedness, she quitted the room, donning the robe as she went.

It was not until she drew near to the door of the Raleigh Chamber that she was able to discern what was being said, for the voices had once again dropped to low tone. As the footman had adjourned to his quarters and there was no one abroad to witness her action, Sharonne took the liberty of placing a discreet ear to the door in order to get the gist of the conversation, which could not be termed sociable in any sense of the word.

"And precisely what figure do you have in mind?" her husband was rasping acidly.

"Perhaps something like a hundred thousand will suffice," came the stranger's voice, quite pleasantly.

Bribed! Edmund was being bribed! Why? By whom? Was it someone from his regiment? Had he not resigned his commission after all and this man had come perchance to arrest him, for desertion?

"For how long?" snapped the Marquess.

"Ah, that depends upon how long you wish to guarantee my silence—and her ignorance."

Her? Now whom did he mean—herself? Or some other female that Edmund had possibly known whilst abroad? With her inherent curiosity thus provoked, Sharonne pressed her ear more avidly to the door panel.

"Take your demands to the devil!" was her husband's scathing response. "Even with your guaranteed silence I can't keep it secret for ever. I shall be obliged to tell her eventually."

The visitor seemed unperturbed by the rebuff.

"Zounds! No need to take umbrage, dear fellow, just because your little scheme didn't work out as planned," he commiserated genially. "Although I do indeed sympathise, it is hardly my fault, is it?"

"No, blast you!"

"Tut-tut, Edmund, there is no need to be hostile. After all, I did keep a discreet distance throughout your wedding night, did I not? Egad, if you can't accomplish all you wish in twenty-four hours you certainly aren't the man I deemed you! Here you are comfortably established with titles, wealth, and a doxy who casts Diana in the shade, whilst I have nothing but the Ace of Trumps. But I bear no ill-will—er—as long as we can come to some happy arrangement—"

"I'll see you hang first!"

"Hang? Me—hang? Why should I? What crime have I committed in merely returning to my native soil? 'S blood! Sweet England must surely have fallen to the Barbarians if such is now a hanging matter." He gave vent to an equally barbaric laugh. "Alas, for yourself, dear—er—Edmund, I doubt if the law would view your little escapade quite as leniently. To gull a young innocent wench of good family to the altar so, not to mention masquerading as the fifth Marquess of Ashton . . ." he broke off, clicking his tongue as if chastising a disobedient child. "I feel the rewards could prove rather unpleasant."

Sharonne drew herself up erect with a sharp intake of breath. If her husband were not, after all, Marquess of Ashton, then who was? Gabriel St. Claire? Was he still alive as she had sensed from the outset?

"Now I, on the other hand," resumed the intruder,

"find myself in a position of decided advantage here. 'S life, you must agree, my Lord Marquess," he stressed with irony, "that I'd be several variety of fool not to gather up the golden eggs when the goose has so conveniently laid them at my feet? And I do not consider my demand exorbitant when I have offered to relieve you of your—er—embarrassment."

"I do not wish to be relieved of her!" Edmund rounded on him. "She is not an embarrassment!"

The visitor was not convinced. "Come, come, my good fellow! 'S life, I wonder if she would favour your optimism? A wife who is not a wife *must* be an embarrassment, if not to you, then to herself."

Horror gripped Sharonne. A wife who was not a wife, what could he mean? Did he have the impudence to imply that she and Edmund were not lawfully wed?

"She is an embarrassment to no one until you choose to make her so," retorted Edmund, angrily. "Anywise, where is your proof? How can you verify that she is not my wife?"

"Can you verify that she is?" parried the other calmly. "I arrive in England," he went on, a sinister tone infecting his voice, "to discover some impostor usurping my privileged position and so I decide to investigate. I come to Ashton village and what do I find? I find strange activities afoot at Court St Claire, and even stranger goings on in the chapel yonder."

His privileged position! Was the mysterious caller none other than her arch enemy himself—Gabriel St Claire?

At this terrifying possibility Sharonne leapt away from the door as if it had suddenly struck her, to collide

rather violently with a suit of armour positioned somewhat inconveniently behind.

No matter how manfully she strove to convince herself that the metallic clatter was not so very loud, she
was forced to acknowledge that it was pretty deafening
—without the addition of the scream she had unleashed
as she fell along with it. Consequently, as the last clang
reverberated away through the carved rafters the door
of the Raleigh Chamber was flung wide, and there on
the threshold stood the stranger, gazing down on her in
cynical amusement.

If he were obliged to resemble anyone, Sharonne was
relieved to note, it would be her husband, the only difference between the two being the stranger's broader
stature, coarser complexion and clean-shaven chin—
though he sported as much hair upon his upper lip. In
fact, so relieved was she to discover that the face was
certainly not that of Gabriel St Claire, despite the gentleman's threats to her husband, she permitted him to
assist her from her ungainly sprawl amongst the armour
—whilst she hastily drew the robe over her naked limbs
upon which, she remarked, his vision was quick to
alight. Suddenly a flame of the most virulent jealousy
seemed to flare in his lively blue eyes, but Sharonne
blinked and when next she looked it was gone, leaving
her in doubt about whether she had really seen it at all.

"Well, I do believe it is your delectable Diana, Edmund, eavesdropping at the keyhole," he declared,
pleasantly surprised. "How well you have her schooled.
No—don't flee, my dear," he besought her as she tried
to free herself from his enthusiastic grasp once she had
regained her balance. "Come, join the entertainment! It
is just approaching the peak of diversion."

As he still refused to relinquish his hold, Sharonne had little choice but to accompany him into the room. Once inside he released her and closed the door while she rushed across to where her husband stood still clothed in white ruffled shirt and claret breeches, before the great gaping fireplace, his head bowed towards the cold empty grate as he leaned heavily upon the mantelshelf in an attitude of despair, which immediately evoked her concern.

"I'm sorry, Edmund, please forgive me," she begged, placing a compassionate hand on his arm. "I didn't mean to listen at the door, truly! I came down because I heard shouting and thought you were in some danger—"

"You must return to your bed, Sharonne."

"I think not," countermanded the visitor, taking up position by the door.

"Edmund, what is it? H-He seemed to be threatening you," Sharonne appealed to her husband.

"I charge you in all truth, Edmund, was I threatening you?" enquired the gentleman, sauntering into the room to help himself to his host's best burgundy and make his person generally at home as if it were four in the afternoon instead of morning, confident in the knowledge that the lady would not attempt to retreat now that her curiosity was coming nicely up to boil.

"You're in no position to threaten anyone," the Marquess flung over his shoulder. "You arrive here in the dead of night alone, with none but one solitary footman to bear witness—"

"Hold hard!" sneered the other through a sudden crack in his affable veneer. "If you have any idea germinating in that infernal mind of yours to have me beaten over the head and walled up in your wine-cellar, my good man, let me at once dispel it. I have lodged at The Weaver's Arms this sennight past and ingratiated myself with the surrounding tenantry. Alack, should anything untoward occur they might take it sorely amiss, especially as my reckoning has not yet been paid."

"How dare you insinuate that my husband would do such a heinous thing, sir!" Sharonne rounded on the stranger. "This is *his* house, and you are here merely on tolerance as an uninvited guest. Who do you think you are to presume so much?"

"Well, Edmund?" prompted the gentleman with infuriating sang-froid. "Who am I? Come, we are all agog!"

As her husband seemed reluctant to answer, Sharonne turned back to address the visitor and thereby fill the breach.

"Are you perchance in the army, sir?" she questioned with asperity.

"Forsooth, ma'am!" he acquiesced with a bow. "You are extremely perceptive. In spite of mine efforts to mimic the common civilian garbed thus in my russet broadcloth, you detect the soldier beneath."

"And if you would deign to answer my next question in all honesty I—"

"Egad, mistress!" exclaimed he, devoured with feigned anguish. "How could I be false to one so fair?"

Sharonne deemed him to have managed passing well thus far.

"Have you come here to arrest my husband? Perhaps for deserting his post?"

The stranger's response was to throw back his dark

head and give full licence to a loud rumbling belly-laugh.

"Nay, ma'am," he chortled, dabbing at his eyes with the end of his linen stock. "Though, damme, dear Edmund might wish it were indeed so, eh, Edmund?"

Sharonne thought it would have been too good to be true also, for her stomach was beginning to churn with foreboding that the truth was going to affect her a deal more personally than a case of military insubordination, which did not explain away the clash of opinion regarding the marriage.

Meanwhile the visitor lounged at his ease upon a day-bed, studying the Marquess who continued to ignore his banter.

"Gad, what a plaguey hang-dog fellow you are!" he observed at length. "I could spirit her off from under your supercilious nose and I'd warrant you'd not raise a finger to stop me."

"Edmund," Sharonne petitioned her husband for the truth, for she doubted exceedingly if she would ever ascertain it from the guest. "Who is this man? Why do you allow him to address you in this uncivil manner?"

"Well, Edmund?" supported the gentleman, unruffled. "Do you accede to my request? Or do I accede to the lady's natural curiosity?"

With a further pang of alarm Sharonne noticed her husband manifesting one by one all the warning signs of fomenting rage which prompted her to round upon the cause once again.

"Why dost thou seek to persecute my husband so? What has he done to merit such evil intent? I suggest you take yourself back from whence you came, sir, or I shall have no alternative but to have the servants eject you by force!"

"Gadzooks, mistress! You do me grave injustice!" spluttered the gentleman, bobbing up indignantly. "Though you evidently don't appreciate it, I stand firmly on your side!"

"Then you must be on my husband's side also."

"I swear, I shall take mine unwelcome self off out of your sight the instant dear Edmund here sanctions my proposition."

The Marquess finally rounded on the visitor, battling to rein in his temper.

"I will never agree to your extortion if you haggle till the crack of doom! Here!"—he seized Sharonne by the arm and dragged her bodily across the room to confront the man. "There's my wife! Tell her, damn you!" he exploded furiously, striking terror into the heart of Sharonne who had never seen him thus enraged before.

A look of mordacious hatred distorted the visitor's swarthy visage upon realisation that his host was not going to be beaten into submission. But this he managed to suppress, to echo with a mocking laugh:

"Your wife! I do declare you make exceeding free with the term."

"Take care what you say, sir," Sharonne flashed venomously. "I think you would imply that my husband and I are not lawfully wed."

"Precisely, ma'am," quoth he, unperturbedly. "In fact, I might even presume to say that you are as much my wife as his."

Sharonne gasped aloud at the gentleman's sheer effrontery.

154

"H-How dare you! How dare you say such a dreadful thing! Edmund, give him the proof he requires. Throw his disgusting insinuations back in his face by proving once and for all that we are indeed man and wife!"

This, oddly enough, Edmund seemed loath to do.

"Come now, Edmund, don't be perverse," seconded the gentleman with a sneer. "Present your proof, or kindly present me to *our* wife."

"Present yourself!" snapped the Marquess.

"Uncouth dog!" retorted the other with contempt. "Can I do aught to better it if your accurst conscience decides to rear its unsavoury head at the crucial hour, denying you the Elysian pleasures you crave?"

"Sir!" Sharonne cried, floundering in all this ambiguity. "How can I be wed to you, when I am already wed to my husband yonder?"

The visitor took a veritable age to rise from the day-bed, then stood appraising her from head to toe, a lascivious smile playing round his lips.

"You married Edmund St Claire, did you not?"

She repaid his question with a look of confusion. "Yes, well?"

"Then you must be wed to me, ma'am, for I am he," he informed her with a flourishing bow. "Lord Edmund William John Augustus St Claire, at your service."

Sharonne was stunned, humiliated and outraged, in that order, before she verbally attacked him, beginning to suspect the man incapable of uttering one word of truth.

"Y-You can't be! Y-You're an imposter, sirrah! A liar! A scoundrel! A—"

"Avast, ma'am, I readily acknowledge one of us to be an impostor! However, I do swear on solemn oath that 'tis not I."

A strange sensation that the man might well be genuine in his avowal began to assail Sharonne, even as she turned for confirmation to her husband.

"Edmund, tell me that this man lies," she pleaded in desperation, hastening across to gaze up wild-eyed and distraught into his expressionless face, raking his eyes for the vital answer she so feverishly sought. "Prove to me that he is indeed the impostor!"

But no answer of any kind was forthcoming as he turned away from her and meandered back to the fireplace where, drawing himself up to his full height, he raised a hand to his chin, and to his wife's abject horror, tore off the beard, likewise the moustache, and cast them aside—after which, he unhurriedly removed the tight curling wig from his head, and allowed the shower of blond silken hair to tumble down about his shoulders, revealing in all his arrogant beauty, who else, but Gabriel Francis Louis Philippe St Claire, the fourth Marquess of Ashton?

7

No! No! No! mouthed Sharonne soundlessly, slowly pivoted her head from side to side, as if this alone would transform the man before her abhorrent gaze into someone, or something, else. Anything! Anything but his execrable self! Anything, rather than be forced to acknowledge the plain unadulterated truth and release the floodgates of crucifying pain and heartache already battling for recognition. No, her Edmund couldn't be Gabriel St Claire, never! He had loved her! All these past months he had loved her—or had he? He had never said so. She had loved him; oh, yes, that was incontestible. But perhaps she had loved him too much, to the exclusion of all else, including reason, until she was obsessed by her overwhelming passion to the point of blindness—blind to his defects, his diabolical treachery. Oh, what a fool she had been—a poor, blind, crazed fool! Her father had sensed his hypocrisy, had tried to open her eyes to the truth and save her from this dire fate. Oh, how abominably she had repaid her poor dear father!

"Sweet, sweet revenge! Oh, bitter-sweet revenge!" a small voice cried within her heart as by degrees the agony of realisation made itself felt, welling up inside her until she had to battle valiantly to quell an overpowering urge to scream, scream, and never stop! To tear out her hair in huge handfuls and rampage through the house smashing everything in sight!

How she hated him! Oh, how she truly hated him!

Never had she hated so intensely before—but yes! When she had lain across her brother's lifeless body that fatal morning in Hyde Park she had indeed hated him.

Sharonne backed further and further away from him, as far as she possibly could, her face distorted with a sickening revulsion, back and back until she felt the sturdy figure of Lord Edmund behind her. Instinctively his arm went about her shoulders, protectively, to which Sharonne did not take exception despite the fact that she had known him barely thirty minutes. She was sorely in need of comfort, someone—anyone—to turn to in this her hour of direst need, and Lord Edmund chanced to be on hand, ready and only too willing to give the necessary succour. Indeed, who was in a better position to give this solace than the man she had until this tragic hour believed herself in love with? The man she had believed herself married to? And, most important of all, the man who had unwittingly saved her from sacrificing the greatest gift she had to offer, the ultimate, her honour! How much more unbearable would her plight have been had Lord Edmund St Claire happened to thunder upon the door just a few simple seconds later . . . ? A shiver ran through her shattered frame, her back cleaving to Lord Edmund as if seeking to draw upon his abundance of strength to sustain her through the hours of blackest despair which lay ahead. Oh, how she had gravely misjudged this man whom she now believed had been sent, guided, by Providence to her side this night. How was she to even begin apologising for her execrable accusations and insults? For threatening to have him forcibly ejected?

"Permit me to escort you to your room, ma'am," he

murmured of a sudden, as if sensing her delicate condition. "You have sustained a severe shock. I shall order a hot posset be sent up to you directly."

"I—I am quite r-recovered, m-my lord," she faltered —seeming to give the lie to this by trembling and clinging to his arm the harder whilst struggling to rally all her resources to get out of the room with dignity, no matter if she collapsed afterwards upon the stairs. "Th-thank you for your kind offer, but I-I'd prefer to go alone. G-Good night."

The door closed and she was gone, leaving the brothers strangely silent when only half an hour ago they seemed to have so much to say.

"Well, Gabriel?" enquired Lord Edmund anon. "Are you satisfied with this outcome? Is your thirst for revenge finally appeased to see her thus cast down? In truth, you must experience a great fulfilment to see your meticulous planning and contriving brought to such triumphant fruition."

The Marquess bore his gibes with admirable fortitude.

"Come, brother, pray tell me how she comes to merit such punishment?"

"And replenish your store of powder and shot?" countered the Marquess blisteringly.

"Very well, I'll hazard a guess and merely assume that she has pinked you in your most vulnerable spot —your pride," went on Edmund, undaunted. "But what of *her* pride? What is to become of her now? Or is it also part of your plan that she should languish and die of a broken heart over this mythical Edmund? Or perhaps make an end of her shame and humiliation by drowning herself in yonder lake?"

Lord Ashton held his peace with superhuman control, his long tapering fingers gripping the mantelshelf until his knuckles glowed white with the strain, adamantly refusing to cede to his brother's feverish interest.

"Hm-m, from my view she has a choice of two courses," resumed his guest, attacking from another vantage point as he gazed idly round the wainscotting and tasteful furnishings of the Raleigh Chamber. "She can humble herself to her father, or seek employment of some kind. But I think she will adopt neither of these. I wager she will adopt a third course—namely, myself."

Lord Ashton swung round from the fireplace, eyes blazing.

"By the death! What cunning ploy is this?"

"Ecod! Where cunning ploys are concerned, brother, you leave us all gawping at the starting post!" retaliated Lord Edmund. "As she is readily available, I shall woo her and wed her in all honour. After all, she is wed to me in name, therefore—"

"She is wed to you in nothing! The ritual was a complete travesty from start to finish! No banns, no licence —even the parson was bogus!"

His brother flung him a look of scathing contempt. "Never did do anything in half-measures, did you, Gabriel? All the same, you are absolutely certain she is still—er—*virgo intacta*?"

The Marquess winced at the painful recollection, "Yes, that too was a farce."

"La, I cannot for the life of me understand why you went to such lengths to arrange all this nuptial chicanery."

"I see no reason whatsoever why I should enlighten

160

you, but she would scarce have deigned to offer me willingly that which I did not wish to take by force."

"Yet you would have me believe the damsel remains unblemished," parried the other, eyes suspiciously narrowed. "Am I to assume, then, that she was still loath to make the offer?"

His brother maintained a grim silence.

"I see," went on Edmund, placing a hand on the doorknob as if about to retire to one of the many chambers above. "Mayhap I shall succeed where you have failed."

"Edmund!" rang out Lord Ashton's voice. "I give you fair warning, if you venture within ten yards of her room I will not spare you!"

"Fret not, dear brother," Lord Edmund smiled pleasantly. "Have not I vowed like a gentleman to wed her in all honour? I trust you do not object? Forsooth, even you yourself could scarce inflict a worse fate upon her, so your thirst for vengeance will be amply assuaged, will it not?"

Meanwhile, Sharonne lay in her bed abovestairs, her entire being numbed by the excruciating shock she had sustained, trying desperately to capture sleep's sweet oblivion which her troubled heart and soul constantly denied her by forcing her to relive the unbearable humiliation of the past months when she had ached and craved for the man who was her bitterest foe and whom she now despised with that same intensity. The man who had deliberately set out to seduce her in this diabolically clever way, playing slowly but steadily upon her most tender feelings with such delicacy of touch, gradually undermining her pride, confidence, self-control, sense of propriety, till she was a pawn in his hands, a weak, helpless slave to his charm, when he might do whatever he wished with her and she unable to say him nay. The man who had cruelly alienated her from her parents, the people she loved and trusted. The man who had sought her shame and downfall by seducing her in the confines of his own home with no place of refuge for her to escape to, had she wished to do so. The man who had married her in a disguise which he could discard whever he tired of her and conveniently assume his true identity, leaving her to bear her terrible burden of shame.

In vain did Sharonne try to prevent her mind returning to Northumberland House, to the wild passion in his eyes which she had, in one moment's delirium, interpreted as love, desire, to realise now in the cold light of day that it had been nought but pure unmitigated hate. But how well he had played his rôle of the gallant swain! How convincing were his kisses and caresses when she must have repelled him beyond endurance. And at her home, surely he deserved the highest commendation for his superb self-discipline during that catastrophic visit?

As the bridal bed should have evoked too many intolerable memories, Sharonne had returned to her former bedchamber, and lay gazing with unseeing eyes at the large mullioned window set high in the opposite wall, oblivious to the initial rays of the early morning sun heralding a new day, her eyes strangely dry, for tears were too inadequate. Thus she lay, dull and lifeless, inwardly congratulating Lord Ashton upon his resounding success. Indeed, he could not have chosen a more fiendish punishment, for she would never be capable of loving anyone again. Her love lay dead at his elegant feet, as Jonathan had done those many years ago, and he was again the acknowledged victor. Yes, she was prepared to admit defeat, prepared to own him far, far more experienced than she at inflicting pain and anguish upon his fellow beings—had not it been his life's work?

But deep, deep down beneath all her recrimination did not a tiny spark of feeling still glow for the Edmund she had known? The Edmund who had that very night loved her with such intoxicating passion to the verge of —no! It had all been trickery! Part of his devilishly clever plot to weaken her resistance and wreak his long awaited revenge. Indeed, if a spark of anything glowed within her for anyone it was of gratitude, overwhelming gratitude to the true Edmund St Claire for arriving at the moment he did and ransoming her soul from everlasting purgatory.

It was this profound gratitude, coupled with the fact that he was the only ally she could now boast in the great house, which gave my Lord Edmund the welcome boost he needed up the ladder of success to Sharonne's heart, for he himself would have been first to acknowledge the fact that where the wooing of the gentle sex was concerned he was not able to hold the proverbial candle to his brother and had relied for the most part upon the attraction of his scarlet uniform. Alas, a degree of heavy handedness was invariably his downfall, and a feverish impetuosity to acquaint himself with what lay beneath the lady's petticoats ere he was done acquainting himself with what was visible above. In this instance, however, nothing was left to chance and Edmund St Claire planned his manoeuvres with all the tactical skill of a military campaign.

He allowed Sharonne three full days to languish undisturbed in her room, and upon the fourth—when she had every intention of remaining thus closeted for a month, if not the rest of her life—he made his initial overture. This was, despite his brother's direct warning, up to her boudoir door to call softly, coaxingly, pitifully, through the keyhole, hoping to generate some kind of emotion in her stricken heart. Obviously he did not expect success at the first attempt and upon being requested—though in the most courteous manner—to take himself off, he did so without the slighest offence.

After three such rebuffs he changed his strategy and undertook to melt her indifference with a gift or two, nothing of immense value but trivial items which females seemed to set such store by, namely, posies of wild flowers, knots of ribbons, little delicacies of marchpane to tempt her palate when she refused to eat, or a simple sonnet in keeping with her mood.

During this while Sharonne sat idle in body but not in mind as she realised with sudden stark appreciation that some effort would need to be made to prepare for whatever future she had left to her. It was now that she fully understood her parents' erstwhile anxiety at the way in which she had frivolously spurned bachelor upon eligible bachelor, for with the reality of loneliness and destitution staring her bleakly in the face love, somehow, seemed to dissolve into the realms of fantasy, outpaced by necessity.

No, she was not in any position to spurn a man like Lord Edmund, nor any other. He was tall, dark and debonair, and though a younger son was nevertheless a lord and of tolerable circumstance even if the title were purely a courtesy one. Indeed, a maid in her dire plight at the advanced age of almost twenty-four could hardly do worse. Furthermore, she was reputedly wed to him already and her reputation would not suffer to any alarming degree. And if his elder brother did happen to erupt from the grave, alive and well, then it was no fault of Lord Edmund's. Moreover, he was fully aware of her awkward situation and that despite external appearances she was yet unblemished—and if she were prepared to admit to the particle of longing she secretly cherished for the Edmund she had known, surely the true Edmund St Claire was the best available substitute? Indeed, she could never hope to find a man who resembled him more closely, therefore it was reasonable to assume that in time she would grow to love him just as intensely.

Consequently, Lord Edmund St Claire's dedicated efforts finally met with a modicum of success when next he appeared at the keyhole, and ere very long had ingratiated himself sufficiently in her favour to be permitted to attend her levee and breakfast with her each morning. One week later, this had graduated to riding around the estate together, strolling in the gardens, or if the weather proved inclement, playing cards and suffering her to entertain him with her torturous renderings upon the harpsichord—to his simulated delight. Upon other occasions she would thrill to tales of his wild adventures abroad, of the countries he had seen, and the battles he had fought under the great Clive.

Indeed, Sharonne warmed to him so readily she wondered why she had elected to keep to her room so long, though dubiously owned her prime reason for so doing to have been on account of the Marquess and the dire dread which consumed her heart at the very possibility of being obliged to face him again. But upon finally abandoning her chamber she appreciated how unfounded were her fears, for the Marquess seemed to be equally loath to encounter her if the way he never once set foot outside of his private apartments at the opposite end of the house was aught to go by.

Why, she could no quite determine, but as days passed her initial relief at not having to confront him gradually ceded to curiosity regarding his opinion of her as a sister-in-law—for Lord Edmund made no secret of the fact that he would have her for his bride as soon as she felt equal to the occasion, but trusted she would not make him wait too long as he was anxious to quit Court St Claire for a more genial atmosphere. In truth, why she should make him wait at all was something Sharonne could not comprehend, for she was persuaded to agree that there was little purpose in postponing the marriage. After all, it was not as if she had suffered a bereavement, even if it felt like it.

The time she expended in Lord Edmund's company was not absorbed entirely in idle chit-chat. It proved to be an invaluable opportunity to probe the heart and mind of this man whom she had already vowed to marry, for as yet she knew extremely little about him. But to her disconcertion, Sharonne found that no matter what topic of conversation she introduced, or how she introduced it, ere long Gabriel would become the dominant factor, for Edmund seemed wholly unable to discuss anything whatsoever without the influence of his elder brother manifesting itself to such an inordinate degree that he was quite clearly obsessed by him. For a while she humoured him in this and very soon detected precisely which way the wind blew, evident in the bitter resentment which surged up in Edmund at the manner in which Gabriel had been indulged all his life, fêted and fawned upon, whilst he was ignored. This pale, delicate, angelic brother who had constantly been acclaimed as some immortal god, and at whose feet the entire family did regular homage! His unparagoned beauty which had drawn the fair sex in their languishing hundreds—even as a boy—to cosset and fondle him like some new breed of lap-dog. Only he, Edmund, the outcast brother, was able to perceive the innate evil in him, the fiend growing inside him, destined one day to utterly devour him body and soul, and prove his destruction! But no one would pay heed to his grim prognostications. Instead, they accused him of jealousy—jealousy! Oh, how he *hated* brother Gabriel!

This, it would appear, was Edmund and Sharonne's great common bond, the bond which had drawn them together and which would unite them in holy wedlock, to wit, their mutual abhorrence of Gabriel St Claire. A sound basis for marriage, some might think, for is it not as intense, passionate, as love? However, my Lord Edmund sought not only to impress upon his future bride how much *he* hated his brother, but how much he deemed *she* must hate him also, as if he were experiencing some difficulty in reconciling the insane love she had cherished for him as 'Edmund' with her insane hatred for him as himself, for was he not one and the same man?

Sharonne certainly had to make no pretence of hating the Marquess. She hated him beyond reason! This pleased Edmund, and when she went on to reassure him that she would do all in her power to make him a good wife and assuredly grow to love him in time, he seemed quite satisfied, almost happy . . . for a while, until the name of Gabriel erupted again in their discourse, causing Sharonne to wonder if she were reiterating her hatred of the Marquess purely to convince her prospective spouse?

It was a natural reaction for her to compare the two loves she had known, the tenderness of one and the bubbling aggression of the other; the gentle caress and the rough grabbing; the ardent embrace and the bear hug; and, most of all, the soul-stirring kiss of the former, and the lip-bruising of the latter. And although the old Edmund had never actually declared his love for her (indeed, she now knew why) he had, nevertheless, made her feel wanted, needed desperately, even if it was generated by a most ulterior motive, whereas with Lord Edmund she had the uncomfortable feeling that he was eager to wed her solely to spite his brother in some strange perverted way.

Howbeit, in all fairness it must be said, throughout the three short weeks following the disruption of Sharonne's life my Lord Edmund conducted himself with admirable decorum. Not once did he presume to take advantage—though he was given ample opportunity—apart from the occasional embrace and kiss which, far from transporting her into raptures as his counterpart's had done, left her feeling quite unmoved. This, of course, was due entirely to her present state of shock, and once she had fully recovered from the past and the fact that Gabriel St Claire was alive and did not intend to wreak any further vengeance upon her, undoubtedly Edmund's kisses and embraces would thrill her as never before. Moreover, upon reflection, perhaps it were wiser to quit the house as soon as possible, for whilst the spectre of the man she had loved continued to hover round her she could not expect to develop a similar love for her new husband-to-be.

Then why did she continue to procrastinate? Why did she invent excuse upon excuse to remain at Court St Claire as if it were already her home and contained fond remembrances instead of the tragic events she would as lief forget? Why did she no longer fear Gabriel St Claire, her arch enemy? And why did not she rush upstairs in frenzied haste to pack her effects and be off with Edmund, far, far away from Gabriel's malicious intent? After all, she could hardly wish to endure in such proximity to him, to continue living thus in his house when he had murdered her brother and abused her person so heinously! Therefore, one can only assume that this strange reluctance was due to the fondness she yet nurtured for the old Edmund, the Edmund she had loved so desperately and who was now the spirit impregnated in the Gothic walls of the great house in place of Gabriel St Claire, the man who had usurped his place as the living being. But he could never usurp his place in her heart, could he?

8

IT WAS all arranged. On the Friday of that week Sharonne would journey to London with her future husband and there they would be wed as soon as preparations could be made. It was assumed that the Marquess would not be attending the wedding, for the announcement of it had evoked not the slightest response from him, where he yet remained cloistered in the hallowed precincts of his chambers, and whom Sharonne had not seen nor spoken to since the fateful night of Edmund's arrival.

That fateful night! Throughout the past weeks she had forbidden her mind to encroach upon this precarious ground, for whenever she allowed it to do so she was suddenly overcome with the most consummate guilt as if the whole passionate episode had been founded upon sincerity instead of the foul deceit she knew it to be. It was not until this eleventh hour that she chose to liberate her mind, to let it relive every moment from her arrival at Court St Claire, asking herself why he had failed to take fullest advantage of the actual wedding night when she had lain abovestairs helplessly in his power, utterly at his mercy? Surely this night should have seen the whole culmination of his plan? The moment he had suffered and striven for over the previous months, years? Had driven like the devil incarnate to his house, and wed her that very night in such a frenzy of haste it almost seemed he feared his supply of hatred might evaporate before he had time to realise his objective.

What had gone amiss? Why had not he expended the entire night cruelly seducing her? Debauching her in a passion of hate? Crushing her heart in his long white fingers and trampling her love contemptuously underfoot? Why? Why? She had reproached him! Provoked him! Begged and cajoled him! Yet he had not come . . . until the following night. Yes, he had eventually come, though not to debauch nor share her, but instead to love her, to love her with a clean heart, a pure wholesome love—this she was compelled to admit no matter how strongly she fought to deny it. Love in its truest sense, a thing of profound beauty, excruciatingly beautiful. Oh, why should she now cherish the memory of it thus in her heart? Was it perhaps because these were the last rapturous moments she had shared with Edmund, *her* Edmund? And now that he was Gabriel, did she truly love him any less? Yes! Yes! Of course she did! How could she possibly thrill so to the man she hated most in all the world? And if she were to see him again, now, would she indeed hate him as she had done all these years? Yes! Yes! Of course she would! Nothing had changed; he was the same man, she the same woman, and Jonathan the same lifeless thing!

Then why did she not go and seek out the Marquess of Ashton? No! Why not? If she did not fear he would harm her, then what precisely did she fear? Nothing! She would prove it! She would seek him out and lay the ghost of the old Edmund to rest for all eternity. She would prove that her love for him was quite, quite dead. She would gaze once again upon that angelic-evil

171

face and prove categorically that her hatred still burned as fiercely as ever!

Suddenly it was all-important that Sharonne fulfil this vital need, as if her entire future were suspended upon it. It was Wednesday noon and Edmund had ridden off to Dorchester for the day upon some errand—she would never be granted a more opportune moment in the two remaining days. However, she could scarcely invade the Marquess's privacy in such forthright manner without first concocting some plausible excuse for so doing. Therefore, she decided to extend the proverbial olive branch and make her peace with him, for it was as good an excuse as any when they were soon to be related. Granted, they might not become friends exactly, but there was no reason why they should not be able to face each other across the dinner-table like civilised mortals.

Her plan thus formulated, Sharonne then deemed it politic to phrase a few apposite words together in some kind of speech, taking extreme care not to touch upon anything which could prove inflammatory in any way. Once this was composed and memorised to her satisfaction, she betook herself aloft to knock with commendable resolution upon the door to my lord's rooms in the east wing of the house, then stood apprehensively by awaiting some response, reciting her speech under breath whilst her heart accelerated to three times its normal rate.

The valet de chambre eventually answered the call, of whom she politely—nay, humbly—craved audience with his master. The valet bowed and retired, to return almost immediately and inform her, somewhat nonplussed, that his lordship was otherwise engaged and unable to see her. Hastily overcoming her stupefaction, Sharonne civilly acknowledged this and retreated, for there seemed to be little else she could do. Something, she could not quite determine what, suddenly collapsed deep within her, for she had not anticipated this cold rejection despite past differences. Obviously, my Lord Marquess did not find it so easy to forgive her as she did to forgive him.

Sharonne returned to the library, unable to reason why she should feel so disconsolate at what had happened, and sank down in the window embrasure to gaze out over the wide expanse of landscaped parkland stretching far into the distance. Her thoughts drifted back over the past tragic years of her life, beginning with her brother's grievous death and her fierce revenge on the Marquess, on to the bitter estrangement with her parents, then the sham wedding and the harrowing loss of the man she had loved, to culminate in this new agony of soul, an agony created by—what? Was it perhaps a combination of all the heartache and tragedy she had suffered, or merely the thought of marrying a man she did not love?

A tear welled in her eye and coursed its lonely way down her cheek as she bethought of the love of the old beloved Edmund and how blissfully happy they might have been had he—

"I understand you wish to see me."

Sharonne started at the unexpected sound of the Marquess's voice, and turned to sustain an even greather shock when her vision alighted upon him where he stood not very far away, his slender fingers gripping a chairback in evidence of the tension consuming his being. But her eyes were adhered to his face in ill-concealed horror at the ghastly change in him, the man who had devastated the world with his peerless beauty, his arrogant airs, and who now stood before her, a wraith of his former self—his complexion, though it had always been pale, of an unnatural greyish tone, his blue eyes heavy and sunken, giving him a gaunt haggard look, while the very bones of his noble countenance seemed about to pierce his flesh.

However, there was no fault to be found in his dress which was as fastidious as always, with the cascading white lace at throat and wrists contrasting strikingly with the rich purple satin of his full-skirted coat trimmed with silver lace, enhanced by a lavender-and-silver waistcoat, while white silk hose graced his shapely legs, silver-buckled shoes his feet, and diamond rings his hands. Nevertheless, it was some time ere Sharonne could make coherent sound as she rose instinctively to her feet to stand with the sun reflecting brilliantly upon her golden head and gown of primrose muslin if she were a golden goddess.

"G-Gab . . . riel . . ." she mouthed, stricken, anon, before rapidly recovering herself. "M-My lord, you have taken me quite unawares," she stammered, at a disadvantage, hurriedly making her curtsy and averting her eyes lest she cause him further embarrassment by continuing to stare so shamelessly.

"F-Forgive me, but I-I did not know . . . I-I mean, no one said that y-you had been taken ill."

"A slight indisposition, nothing more," he assured her, giving the lie to his words by gripping the chairback the harder.

There ensued an intolerable silence whilst Sharonne rattled her brain to recapture the words of her little speech, but at this all-important time they seemed determined to elude her. Nevertheless, she had to say something.

"I-I find I am overcome with reluctance to l-leave your house, Lord Ashton, w-without making some effort to . . . to . . ."

Her voice tailed off to an inarticulate whisper, too conscious of his regard to be able to apply her mind to anything further.

"Are you perchance suggesting some kind of reconciliation?" he queried, making no attempt to quell his incredulity.

"Why? Is it too much to ask, my lord?" parried she.

"No, but who is to crave forgiveness of whom? Who is the oppressed, and who is the oppressor?"

Sharonne cleared her throat apprehensively to propose tentatively: "I-I thought perhaps a kind of mutual agreement would suffice. For example, if you would give me your assurance that you will seek no further revenge—"

"I've already given my word that you have nought to fear of me, if you recall . . . ?"

Yes, she now recalled the promise he had made on that night, that momentous night.

"I-In return I shall promise likewise."

"I am relieved to hear it. I declare, I am in no fit condition to survive another ordeal of your contrivance."

Neither was she able to survive another of his, but she refrained from saying so, for he looked so delicate she feared he might crumble before her eyes and for some strange reason she was suddenly anxious to spare him, to protect him as one would a sick child.

"W-Was the King's Navy such a terrible ordeal, my lord?" she probed with discretion, not certain if he wished to have the distasteful topic raised.

"The King's Navy? No, that I may well have borne, though 'twas not what I had been accustomed to, I grant you."

Sharonne stared at him in some bewilderment. "W-Were you not in the King's Navy, Lord Ashton, all those years?"

He threw her a cynical sidelong glance and moved two paces further away as she ventured two paces nearer.

"No, Miss Falconer! Your endeavors were not in vain. Your brother's death was handsomely avenged, you have my word on't."

"You knew then that 'twas I?"

He inclined his head in marked agreement. "True, you had me gin-sodden, but I was not completely unconscious. I did not fail to recognise the voice, though my vision was somewhat impaired."

"I-I'm sorry, my lord."

The Marquess flashed her a suspicious glance, no more surprised than Sharonne herself, who could think of no feasible reason for apologising.

"Sorry? For what?" he exclaimed. "For my degradation? My suffering which you so expertly arranged? 'Pon my soul, do not ruin the effect by admitting defeat so early in the game. The best is yet to come! Pray be seated, mistress! Seven years of mine existence cannot be related in seven seconds—though I shall endeavour to be brief."

Sharonne lowered herself dubiously on to a high-backed settee, not sure if she genuinely wished to hear what had every prospect of being a rather unpleasant tale. She had intended he should suffer, yes, as Jonathan had suffered, but that was seven years ago. A great deal had come to pass since then when she had been a gullible child of sixteen, and although Jonathan, her dead brother, would never be forgotten, the whole sordid incident had somehow slowly faded into obscurity —until the advent of 'Edmund'.

"My career in His Majesty's Navy lasted almost three years," he resumed amicably, establishing himself upon the corner of a tortoiseshell-and-gold inlaid writing desk, "though I must surely have been the most unwilling servitor in naval history. Even so, upon reflection, it compares quite favourably with my subsequent fate, however distasteful I deemed it at the time. In fact, when were blown off course along the African coast and challenged by privateers I viewed it as a blessed release. But, alas, they proved to be no better than the tribal races and slaughtered the weaklings, preserving the rest for their own devious gain. Needless to say," he emphasised with irony, "I was considered a weakling but was obligingly spared, for my hair and skin had by now reverted to their original colour, and fair slaves bring a high price."

A gasp of revulsion erupted from his listener. "S-Slaves?"

Lord Ashton smiled his acquiescence. "I was sold into bondage, though, I hasten to add, not to any ordinary master, for I was no ordinary slave! No, I was reserved for a most distinguished master, a Moroccan potentate, no less! La, with an harem of some hundred wives to keep him entertained, one might have presumed him to number amongst the privileged few of this lamentable world to know the meaning of content-ment—but no! My Prince was prone to the melancholy. He wanted his boredom relieved, and desired me to relieve it. I was regarded as something of a novelty, a freak of nature with the fairness of one sex and the body of the other. Forsooth, methinks I cost him dear! Consequently, he was put sorely out of countenance when I rebelled against his—er—overtures—"

"Overtures, m-my lord?" faltered Sharonne, not daring to credit the interpretation battling for precedence in her naïve mind—which the Marquess did not choose to confirm.

"—and so he sought to persuade me."

"Persuade you? H-How?"

His lips curled caustically. "As only the Arab races knoweth, Miss Falconer. Indeed, they are extremely adept at persuasion. Their methods, though a trifle unorthodox, are highly effective!"

Sharonne gulped hard. "Y-You weren't . . . t-tortured?" she stammered, appalled.

"Forgive me if the intelligence offends your sensibilities. Rest assured, I derive no enjoyment from the revelation, for I scarce emerge with credit. I seek simply to stress your resounding success," he clarified suavely.

A pang seared her soul, for neither would she emerge with credit if he truly believed her to be drooling with relish over his harrowing tale, even if he was Gabriel St Claire, the man she was supposed to loathe and despise.

"However, it may detract a trifle from your satisfaction to know that I did not yield . . . though I oft-times wondered . . . if I chose . . . the wiser course. . . ."

"Oh, Gabriel!" she breathed in anguish, despite his opinion of her. "D-Did you suffer much?"

He could not forgo a tremulous smile at the question.

"No more than I could withstand, even if it did require the assiduous ministrations of three physicians to set me to rights—though, appreciably, I still bear some evidence, both spiritual and physical. Happily my face was spared, not in any generosity to me, but to my illustrious master who commanded his villainous dogs to preserve my beauty in deference to his desire."

A shiver of the utmost repugnance ran through Sharonne. If he observed this he gave no indication of it whilst he wandered round the well-stocked bookshelves, his eyes travelling their length as if unable to believe that he was actually in his beloved old home and the ghastly occurrences he pictured so vividly in his mind were indeed all in the past.

"Although 'tis all of two years agone, I find myself yet plagued by the most realistic . . . hall . . . ucin . . . ations."

"P-Please, m-my lord, I beg you! S-Say no more—"

"Why, pray? Surely the knowledge of my excruciating suffering can bring you nought but the most exhilarating pleasure? Your revenge was abundantly realised. Was not this your most ardent ambition?" This was not uttered with the faintest breath of sarcasm, but in deadly earnest.

"No! I—I mean, yes—at that time, seven years ago," she cried, racked with remorse.

"And now?" he pursued with interest. "Faith! I trust you do not now repent of your action, for 'tis somewhat late in the day, you must agree, and all my tribulations will be set at nought!"

A slight frown momentarily disfigured Lord Ashton's classic forehead, for it was quite apparent by her very expression and demeanour that this would indeed seem to be the case. But the Marquess was no more perplexed by this reaction than Sharonne herself who, according to the Law of Nature and the evidence confronting her, really ought to have experienced the greatest elation for, as my lord had fully stressed, was not this the very goal she had striven to attain? Yes, her enemy had been amply punished for his heinous deed in slaying her brother, this she readily admitted—but where was the satisfaction? Why was she prey to more intolerable agony of soul than upon that disastrous night when he had revealed his identity, knowing she was responsible for reducing him from the arrogant callous rake to the gaunt, utterly defeated, spectral figure before her, this shadow of his former self? Why should her conscience thus deny her the peace of mind which surely was her right? Was it not diabolically unjust that she also should suffer the misery and pain which was rightfully his to bear? That she must be pierced with unbearable anguish every time she glanced at him . . . and yet, in a strange spiritual way, never had he looked more dangerously appealing, so ethereally beautiful as in his present weakness, with a long tress of flaxen hair gently caressing his wan cheek, playing havoc with her maternal instinct to nurse him, cherish him back to his customary health—and his eyes! Those dark-ringed, long-lashed, soul-torturing eyes set in that fragile countenance. Eyes which nervously deviated round his surroundings the while in a concerted effort to evade her gaze.

"I must emphasise, Miss Falconer, that I was reared

in the lap of luxury. Such harsh treatment has ne'er been mine unhappy lot. Nevertheless, it pleaseth me to note that I bore up as bravely as most, though p'raps not as bravely as I might. . . ." Again he drifted into the past, a pained expression marring his features—to rally himself, as if suddenly recalling her presence. "Countless times did I beseech my Maker to release me with a merciful death, but it was constantly denied. He ordained that I should live, and so sustained me. But that which sustained me most of all was the hope I feverishly cherished of one day wreaking mine own particular vengeance upon the instigator of my suffering, to wit—yourself!"

He now took to pacing the floor, the memory of his injustice no doubt infusing in him a new strength—though cautiously preserving a distance from where she sat not far from the window with the afternoon sun creating a halo about her head.

"Every death-defying pain and humiliation inflicted on me was alleviated by the thought of how to claim retribution if my chance finally came, and come it did! I created such a fever of jealousy in wifely bosoms that his entire harem assisted eagerly in my escape. They acquired me money, suitable raiment, and even a passage to England! The moment of atonement was fully come!"

Again he paused, this time to regale himself with brandy from the collection of decanters housed in a Japanese lacquered cabinet.

"My plan was to seek you out, seduce you, debauch you, reveal my identity and with hellish delight reject you! Obviously, had you been already wed I should have adapted my methods accordingly. All went exceptionally well—as you are already aware—though I was obliged to implement the wedding. Granted, I may have managed well enough without. In fact, it would have been a deal simpler to have carried you off against your will and ravished you at my pleasure; however, this would have afforded me nought but a brief satisfaction. No, I had to make you love me—it was vital! I wanted everything you had to give, everything! I had to own you body and soul, but most of all, I wanted your heart —desperately, to mangle as you'd mangled my pride! My self-respect! My entire being!"

He broke off, leaning heavily on the cabinet, consuming yet another glass of spirit to quell the battle raging within him.

"Then came the final stage—my moment of frenzied triumph! The moment I had sacrificed my blood, almost my very life for! And to my utter self-disgust I found I couldn't see it through. Would you credit it? All that accursed time I'd expended suffering and plotting in that living hell—not to mention dancing attendance on you like a lovelorn idiot, moulding you to my will—and when the vital moment came to claim my rewards 'fore God, I couldn't do it! And do you know why?" He rounded on her suddenly from the cabinet, glass in hand, his eyes blazing in passionate remembrance. "Oh, do pay heed, mistress, for this is the choicest part of my narrative, guaranteed to send you into transports! Do you have the remotest idea why I couldn't touch you?"

"N-No, my l-lord," she stammered uncomfortably.

"Because I found my vengeance thwarted by love! Love! Me, Gabriel St Claire—in love! And not with just any female, faith no! I had to be in love with my sworn enemy—you, Miss Falconer! Yes, incredible is it not?" he exclaimed with searing contempt. "Well? Please feel at liberty to chortle an you so wish! I must confess, I should not hesitate to do so myself were it not so . . . damnably . . . path . . . etic."

His voice broke and he had swift recourse to his glass as he flung away, striving to regain his self-control.

Sharonne, contrary to his supposition, felt no greater inclination to laugh than he. In fact, it required all her will-power to stop herself from bursting into tears.

"If I acted somewhat discourteously that night, I crave your pardon," he murmured, choked with emotion. "I wanted to consummate the marriage as much as you, but knew it to be a sham. I despised myself intensely, both for arranging it and for not fulfilling it. I was torn apart, detesting you one minute and loving you to distraction the next."

He pulled up short to check his errant steps and, rather than pass close by her, circumvented his path around the three-foot globe of the world established in the centre of the room.

"By the following night my position was quite clear, likewise my feelings. My soul was purged of all hatred and all that remained was a devilish heartache as I realised what you truly meant to me." He flashed her an apologetic look. "Though you will be disinclined to believe me, Sharonne, I did not venture to your chamber that night intending to seduce you. I came to reason with you, to endeavour to explain the whole sordid business without shocking you out of your mind. But when I saw you lying there in all your breathtaking beauty and soul-destroying innocence my courage failed. I just couldn't risk losing you . . . evoking your wrath and hatred anew."

Sharonne turned her face to the window, her eyes tightly closed, partly to force back the tears and partly to relive that night which, despite all, was a beautiful memory, of something so sacred she was adamantly certain that although they had not been wed in the eyes of the law, they had nevertheless been truly wed in their hearts and minds, for they had indeed been as one.

The Marquess was also rapt in profound thought. Was he too reliving those precious moments? Or was he consumed with remorse and bitter regret for all that had transpired? Regardless of which, he was nonetheless so oblivious to his immediate surroundings that he was quite unaware of Sharonne's soundless approach until he felt her hand upon his arm, and he stiffened, instinctively.

"Don't touch me, Sharonne, I beg of you," he pleaded hoarsely, at which she stepped hastily back a pace.

"I—I'm sorry, my lord. I did not mean to presume," she apologised, the pain in her voice unmistakable.

"You are to wed my brother, are you not?" he asked with difficulty.

"Yes, we leave for London in two days," she affirmed in hushed tone.

"It is what you wish?"

Well, was it? she was prompted to ask herself—yes, it had to be! She had no choice!

She nodded hesitantly. "Though there is something I would know. . . ."

"Yes?"

"Is there any possibility whatsoever of our being legally wed, Gabriel, you and I?"

"No!" was his peremptory reply, edging away to widen the gap between them. "You may marry Edmund with a clear conscience. Mayhap 'tis for the best. He will bear you hence and banish the past from your mind. Furthermore, you need fear no risk to your reputation for, no doubt, rumours are already circulating round the capital concerning your mutual *tendre*." He was breathing spasmodically, as if labouring under severe strain. "Alas, I cannot obliterate the heartache I've caused you, I cannot give you back the Edmund you knew. I sincerely trust, however, you will be happy with the next best—the real one."

Wretchedness mounted even higher in Sharonne at the gruesome prospect of this future he was ruthlessly outlining for her. Poor Edmund! How was she to be a good dutiful wife to one brother with such terrible remorse burdening her heart for the other? How was she to bid farewell and abandon Gabriel here in all his despair in two short days?

This inspired her to breathe in earnest: "I hope one day you will also wed, my lord. Someone who will truly love you as you deserve."

"I shall never marry," he declared dogmatically, brushing a crease from his whaleboned skirts with an irritable gesture. "There is already one Gabriel St Claire too many in this dismal world. Edmund is welcome to the title and estate, and my blessing on't."

"Lord Ashton! Y-You will not do anything impetuous?" she probed with misgiving at the note of finality in his voice.

"For example, bidding premature adieu to man-

185

kind?" He smiled a bitter smile. "I seldom act on impulse, m' dear, and having survived so much, faith"—he laughed a pathetic version of his old inane laugh, " 'twould be ludicrous, would it not?" He suddenly discarded his facetious vein and with admirable control forced himself to approach her, and taking her hand raised it to his lips. "This must be farewell, my sweet Sharonne," he whispered a little sadly. "I hope you will endeavour to forgive all that has passed between us and perchance think kindly of me sometimes, though I ill deserve it."

"I—I shall never forget you, G-Gabriel," she replied with fervour, wrestling with the outsized lump in her throat.

"Prithee, how am I to interpret such a remark?" he mocked boyishly. "Nay," he gestured her explanation aside. "Allow me to wallow in my conceit, do not shatter the illusion. It contents me to think you mayhap care a little. . . ." He brushed her cheek with a forefinger and it emerged coated with moisture. "Tears, dear one? Not for me, I trust? 'S life, no one has ever shed tears over me—including mine own mother. 'Tis a novel experience."

Again he fell pensive, gazing down upon the hand he still held with a fondness he might have cherished for a pet kitten. In fact, so rapt were the two in their own world that they quite failed to hear a door close and footsteps passing along the corridor outside—to halt abruptly. Neither did they see the look of insane jealousy sweep over Lord Edmund St Claire's sun-kissed face when his passionate gaze alighted upon them in such intimate pose, and as in the chapel during the ceremony he made to take an impulsive step forward, to pause and reconsider, then step back again to watch them furtively while noting further developments.

"You may not be aware of it, Sharonne, nor even care to be," the Marquess was saying abstractedly, "but in spite of everyone I've known, you bear the dubious privilege of having known the true Gabriel St Claire. A pity, you might well have proved my salvation."

He finally relinquished her hand and with a tender pat on her cheek wandered aimlessly over to the door, oblivious to how perilously near he was to receiving a hatchet in his skull from brother Edmund who quickly secreted himself behind a large Chinese vase balanced upon a chest positioned just outside of the door.

"Gabriel!" Sharonne called out suddenly.

Edmund held his breath, bethinking he had been spied, but soon discovered that she nurtured quite another reason for arresting his brother's departure.

The Marquess paused and turned to see Sharonne running towards him as if about to throw herself into his arms when she stopped short in her tracks, obviously stricken with conscience. And overcome with confusion she instead stood fidgeting before him, with eyes modestly lowered.

"I—I'm sorry for all the . . . terrible s-suffering I've . . . c-caused you," she stammered, deeply perturbed. "I—I hope you . . . will also think . . . k-kindly of . . . m-me. . . ."

Whether or not this were all she originally intended to say, alas, would never be known, for one was given the distinct impression that there lay burdened on her heart a great deal more.

187

Lord Ashton continued to study her awhile after her voice petered away, then glanced ceilingwards, heaving a sigh.

"If 'tis any consolation to you at this advanced hour, child, I swear on oath that I never intended Jonathan to die, though obviously I don't expect you to believe me. However, perhaps you might believe my good friend Lord Ravenby, should you ever chance to encounter him."

And with a last brief bow he quitted the room, leaving Sharonne forlorn and dejected as if the sun had suddenly been eclipsed from her world, and my Lord Edmund to glower after his elegant purple-clad figure from behind the T'ang earthenware, a look of indescribable hatred distorting his features.

"Aye, as I warned you once before, my Lord Marquess," he growled savagely to himself. "Enjoy her whilst ye may!"

9

It was some time before Sharonne eventually fell asleep that night, to find her dreams deeply troubled. In fact, they did not seem to be dreams at all, but often stark reality interspersed with the most terrifying nightmares when she would waken trembling and bathed in perspiration, yet overwhelmingly thankful that she had simply been dreaming—or had she? The visions were so vivid, alive. She could even hear the voices quite distinctly. However, it puzzled her that though the dreams differed in actual content they all bore the same theme, of Gabriel and his dire suffering which grew and grew in intensity until he was calling out to her for help, help she was unable to give. She could hear clearly the agony in his voice, see him reaching out to her—but, worst of all, could see the appalling wounds on his body, the scars testifying to the savage mutilations he had endured. And his face, his beautiful face! Someone, garbed all in black, with long skeleton fingers, was bending over him with a red-hot branding iron, about to plunge it into his face. 'No! Not his face!' she heard her own terror-stricken voice scream out in the night, and she sat up with a start, shivering violently, it had all been so very real.

She lay, trembling and gasping in the darkness, relieved to find everything deathly silent throughout the old house with not a solitary voice to be heard, certainly not that of the Marquess. And so she settled down again beneath the comforting sheets, determined

189

not to resume her sleep until she had composed her thoughts lest she resume the ghastly nightmare. But ere long she slept once again.

If she deemed her last dream horrifying beyond measure, alas, there was worse to come, for this time she was in the dark, gloomy chapel of the St Claires—quite alone, or so she believed, for there was not sight nor sound of anyone else. Everything was just as it had been upon the mock wedding night, the same chill feeling, the same sense of foreboding, the same candelabra illuminating the altar, though with an unnaturally bright light of a greenish hue—but wait! There was something else! Something quite large, like a trunk or box of some kind, perhaps a treasure chest, for it was black with gleaming brass fittings. But as she crept nearer she was able to discern in the eerie light that the brass fittings were, in fact, handles of pure gold and that the treasure chest was—a coffin! No, she didn't want to look, refused to look! But some uncanny force was pushing her from behind, compelling her towards the coffin, and she found herself drawn by a gruesome curiosity, nearer, nearer, to see therein—Gabriel, very, very dead!

She screamed a spine-chilling scream but no sound came forth as she gazed upon his pale ghostly features, with the green light shining upon him. He lay in all his regal splendour, adorned in his ermine and velvet robes of state, complete with gold coronet as befitting the second highest peerage in the ranking nobility encircling his head, while his long blond hair draped his shoulders. Granted, the overall scene was fulsomely ghoulish and yet he looked so truly angelic that Sharonne was sorely tempted to kiss those ashen lips and leaned forward—to jump back in alarm as the doors burst back with a resounding bang, and down the aisle clattered and danced Edmund, bedecked in bright scarlet with the horns, forked tail and cloven hooves of Lucifer, and brandishing the familiar three-pronged trident in his hand with which he stabbed at the coffin as he pranced round the funeral bier, shrieking and cackling in wildest glee!

Again Sharonne awoke screaming in the night for him to stop—and once again was she seized with the same ague but overwhelming sense of relief that it was all just a horrid dream. But as before she was consumed with doubts, for now she was wide awake, yet she could hear a voice quite distinctly, yes, it was Edmund's voice, shouting in violent rage, but a distance away belowstairs. And there was Gabriel's more cultured tone, raised to the same volume as he shouted back at his brother, exactly as it had been upon the night of Edmund's advent. Why should they be quarrelling? And at such an unearthly hour?

Sharonne lay listening, tensed, in the darkness, wondering if she were indeed awake and could really hear the voices or if it were a sinister prelude to yet another ghastly nightmare. Should she go downstairs and investigate? This she was naturally loath to do following the disastrous results upon the last occasion! And before she had finished reasoning what action to take, she was once again fast asleep.

This time, she slept quite peacefully. Indeed, she could scarcely believe she had been asleep at all, for she slowly regained consciousness to the same sound, the sound of Edmund's voice, strident and impatient, but in much closer proximity. However, she was not allowed to lie pondering very long before she was shaken quite roughly, almost brutally.

"In Satan's name, wake up, woman!" he was bellowing, enough to waken the dead, if not his bride-to-be. "Get up at once and get dressed!"

"A-At this hour?" she stammered, sitting up to rub her eyes.

"There's been a change in plans, we're leaving."

"I—I beg your pardon?"

"The coach is ready and waiting," he informed her gruffly. "Conduct your toilet and be downstairs in ten minutes!"

"Ten minutes!" she cried indignantly. "I can't be ready in ten minutes, Edmund!"

"Why not? We have everything already packed and stowed upon the coach-box. What do you have to attend to other than yourself?"

Sharonne shrugged, realising the futility in remonstrating with him in his present humour.

"Very well, then would you kindly summon my maid to assist me?"

"You will have to dress yourself, ma'am," he snapped brusquely. "Your maid, I sent off earlier with the rest of the servants. I shall hire you another when we reach London!"

Before she could recover from her astonishment he had slammed the door and stormed off.

Blazing resentment flared up in Sharonne. How dare he take so much upon himself! To literally drag her out of bed at five in the morning and calmly announce that they were leaving twenty-four hours earlier than arranged was more than flesh and blood could stand. Not

192

to mention dismissing the entire household staff without as much as a by your leave. It would be interesting to hear his brother's views on this piece of presumption.

Without more ado, she clambered out of bed and with difficulty (and many unlady-like curses) managed to complete her toilet unassisted, donning the plain lemon cambric gown she had previously set aside for travelling, without a hoop-petticoat for comfort and convenience, and pinning up her hair as best she may into neat though not very becoming coils, rather like a governess, which was the only way circumstance and inexperience permitted.

Once dressed, however, she was assailed with sudden doubt about disturbing the Marquess at such an uncivilised hour, but anon, acknowledged the necessity for drastic action of some kind. There was no alternative, she must needs risk incurring his displeasure.

And so, she betook herself off to the Marquess's apartments as she had dared the previous day, and knocked again upon his door. As she stood waiting for some response she remarked how all was indeed deathly quiet with not a single servant to be seen. She knocked three times more, her heart growing heavier with each knock, wondering why my lord's valet de chambre did not answer. Surely Edmund had not presumed to dismiss him too?

After knocking four times to no avail, she glanced cautiously round, then dared to try the door—to find it locked. Locked? Whom did Lord Ashton wish to keep out of his hallowed chambers?

"What the devil are you doing here?" thundered the unmistakable voice of her future husband at this point, and Sharonne jumped two feet into the air.

"I—I came to b-bid . . . f-farewell to y-your . . . b-brother," she stammered in alarm.

"Is that all you came to give my brother?" he rasped with scepticism. "Your farewells?"

"What else would I give him, Edmund? What do you imply?"

He viewed her through narrowed eyes awhile, then shrugged his suspicions aside.

"It makes no difference. Either way you're too late."

"W-What d'you mean, too late?"

"He's gone."

Sharonne could not suppress a gasp of dismay. "G-Gone? G-Gabriel's gone? Gone where?"

At the expression of obvious disappointment registered on her face, the old insane jealousy swept over Edmund St Claire, the same jealousy Sharonne believed she had seen upon the night he assisted her from amongst the fallen armour, the jealousy she had thought a figment of her imagination—but this time there was no mistake. This time it was so apparent it filled her with a strange sense of danger, especially when related to the horrific dreams she had recently experienced.

"You will return to your chamber at once and pack the rest of your effects!" he roared at her, restraining himself with superhuman control. "After which you will bring them down to the coach!"

"Y-Yes, Edmund," she concurred dutifully, deeming it far wiser to indulge him, for it almost seemed as if he would strike her.

Without further hesitation, she sidled apprehensively past him and hastened back to her room to do his bidding, wondering about this peculiar humour which had fallen upon her espoused and why he should be so suspicious of her and his brother.

It was as she packed her few remaining effects into a band-box that Sharonne's heart weighed heaviest beneath the crucial blow of Gabriel's unexpected departure, and she found it difficult not to forgo a tear at the strong possibility that she might never see him again. Even if she did, Edmund's jealousy was such that he would probably attack his brother in public if he as much as kissed her hand. Oh, how she wished she had known the day before that he too intended quitting Court St Claire—but what difference would it have made? Had he not already bid his adieux to her during their discourse? Was he not his own master, to come and go at will?

With drooping mien she took up her band-box and blue capuchin and progressed slowly to the door, where she returned to cast a last affectionate look around the room—at the curtains of cream damask, the blue hangings, the huge bed with its twisting posts up almost to the stucco ceiling fashioned in scroll and shell patterns, the dressing closet, the fireplace, dresser and its little porcelain figurines and mirror-stand, and the day-bed under the high mullioned window. And swallowing a dry sob, she departed.

The old house gave all appearances of a mausoleum as she descended the stairs, with no sign of any living thing—even Edmund, whom she assumed must have gone outside to the coach—and so she decided to go out too and opened one of the huge doors to pass into the brilliant morning sunshine. There at the entrance, sure enough, stood the coach and six matched bays, but still no evidence of Edmund.

She approached the coach with the intention of bestowing her band-box and cloak inside, but upon opening the door was stunned to find the twin velvet seats piled up with caskets of jewels, gold plate and valuables of every description to such an extreme that there was barely room for anyone to sit!

Edmund was stealing from his own brother! Spiriting away the family treasures behind Gabriel's back. Appreciably aghast, Sharonne hurriedly retraced her steps indoors, though nurturing doubts whether she really ought to confront Edmund with this new development in view of his present mood.

But neither was there evidence of him inside the house as she anon discovered after searching all the main rooms, eventually returning to the Great Hall in some dilemma, debating where to search next, when a muffled thud greeted her ear, and emanating from below her feet—in the cellars. What on earth was Edmund doing in the cellars?

Sharonne immediately made her way to the cellar door to satisfy her curiosity. Even as she approached, a strange aroma assailed her nostrils, and upon opening the door found herself engulfed in smoke. The house was on fire!

"Edmund!" she managed to call down the steps, wafting the smoke aside to get a better view of what was toward. "Edmund! What are you doing down there?"

Edmund appeared on the instant, his face black with fury as it was with soot and grime.

"Now what do you want?" he growled, enraged. "Can't you mind your own blasted affairs? Go, get into the coach and await me without further interference!"

"B-But you need help! The house, i-it's on fire!" she pointed out superfluously, for by now she could hardly see him for smoke and tongues of flame were already lapping hungrily behind him.

"I don't need your confounded help! I'm managing exceeding well alone!" was his contemptuous response.

"Edmund, you'll never put out that fire without help!" she cried hoarsely.

He rapped out a foul oath. "Put it out? Why in hell's name should I be putting it out? It has taken me this hour past to set the infernal thing alight!"

Sharonne gaped, flabbergasted. "It—it's what?" she faltered, experiencing considerable difficulty in comprehending the vile wickedness her future husband was involved in up to his ears. "E-Edmund! Y-you know not what you say . . . I-I must away to fetch help."

Before she had taken two paces towards the door Edmund was up the cellar steps and had her wrist in a grip of iron.

"That, my dear, would be most unwise," he snarled, his fingers almost breaking her arm.

"Edmund, this is wicked! Wicked!" she exclaimed, horrified beyond measure, as precisely what he was about gradually penetrated her numbed senses. "You can't do this diabolical thing to your brother's beautiful home! It's been in your family for two hundred years, it's your heritage! You must stop it! Stop it, at once!"

"Why? What matters one house with titles, fortune and twenty houses at stake?" he flung back at her. "This time I'm going to be Marquess of Ashton, and nobody's going to prevent me—not even you—"

"But it all belongs to Gabriel! Do you honestly expect him to stand by and let you—"

197

"Don't be a fool!" he cut in harshly. "You've nought to thank Gabriel for. You hate him as much as I, don't you? *Don't you?*"

"Y-Yes, Edmund, you know I do," she gabbled hastily, tring to sound convincing as she struggled manfully to free herself, appreciating that the old house with its half-timberwork, hammerbeam ceilings, elaborate fan vaulting and over-abundance of panelling would soon be a blazing inferno.

"Well then? Do not you acknowledge this to be the perfect solution? Some careless menial left a candle burning—'tis a simple enough mishap. No one will suspect foul means!"

"What about your brother?" she reminded him anxiously, marvelling how Edmund could have overlooked the most powerful opposition to his plan. "Surely he will suspect and be justly furious. Edmund—may even kill you!"

If this was designed to discourage him from his evil intent, it unfortunately had the adverse effect. Flinging back his dark head, he gave licence to a long strident laugh.

"Gabriel?" he sneered anon. "He's in no position to kill anyone!"

The most spine-chilling fear gripped Sharonne as she recalled the angry voices in the night and the ghastly dreams, now realising that there had been a deal more reality in them than she had supposed.

Almost too terrified to ask, she forced herself to stammer bravely: "W-Why, Edmund? W-What have . . . y-you done . . . to G-Gabriel?"

He turned a suspicious eye on her. "Do I detect a note of concern, my dear? Do you not now hate my noble brother? Do not you want him dead as he is already reputed to be?"

"Y-Yes, yes!" she cried, but evidently not quite so convincingly this time.

"You lying bitch!" he snarled, tightening his grip on her arm until she screamed with the pain. "It did not look that way yesterday when you were about to throw yourself into his arms! Yes, I saw you!"

"E-Edmund, tell me, I beg you! What vile thing have you done to Gabriel? Where is he?" she shrieked with anxiety, renewing her struggle to gain her freedom.

"Why should it disturb you so, my bride, if you truly hate him?"

"No—I love him! I love him!" she shouted wildly, till it echoed in the high arched rafters.

"How in Satan's name can you love him after what he's done to you?" he rasped with contempt.

"I—I can't explain . . . I—I know I ought to hate him, b-but I can't! I can't!"

"Very well, if you love him so much—find him yourself!" he cackled fiendishly. "You have about five minutes in which to do so before the fire reaches his store of gunpowder. Forsooth, the whole house could go up any minute—it should afford quite a spectacle!"

"You beast! You scoundrel! Let me go!"

Again he gave a burst of raucous laughter. "Don't expect any assistance from him, my dear. If you call out, he will not answer. I brought a pretty little drug with me from the East which I administered to him three hours agone. He lies—though I shan't say where —at this very moment revelling in its rather potent properties."

Sharonne wrestled frantically in his hold and he let her go with a final blood-curdling laugh as thick smoke swirled round their ankles, and the wainscotting in the Great Hall began to char nearest the floor.

But she was free! Free to fly abovestairs to Gabriel's aid, certain he must be in his rooms behind the locked door—as Edmund's hellish laughter echoed round the empty house.

"If you want him you can perish with him, and damnation to you both!" were his final words to her.

Thankful that she wore no cumbersome hoop-petticoat, Sharonne dashed in breathless hast to the Marquess's rooms, aware that the door had been locked, not to keep someone *out* but to keep somone *in*. Oh, how cleverly Edmund had constructed his devil-ish plot, nothing had been left to chance!

Upon reaching the door, she thundered upon it with every physical means at her disposal and screamed his name at the top of her voice. But the door proved to be much stronger than she, and so she ran back to the head of the stairs to seize a stout battle-axe from off the wall with which she launched at the door, hacking and chopping for all she was worth, her sheer determination to save the life of the man she loved endowing her with the abnormal strength she needed so frantically—until the door eventually splintered sufficiently for her to squeeze inside.

Feverishly she swept through all five rooms constitut-ing his personal apartments, aghast to find no one there! Again she searched each room in turn, unable to stop herself crying out his name although he was sup-posedly unconscious, but all to no avail. Smoke was al-ready penetrating the upper floors as she dashed from room to room, coughing and searching madly, but, alas, was soon obliged to abandon her search, for the smoke was choking her—she must turn back or perish! All she could now do was return to Edmund and beg him to disclose his brother's whereabouts before it was too late—she would offer him anything in desperation, and beg on her bended knees! But how could she trust him to tell the truth? He had arranged all this with meticulous precision for his own devious gain; why should he help her jeopardise it? Was Gabriel in the cellars? Had Edmund perchance done him cruelly to death in the night and—oh, no! Please God—no! she prayed wildly as she fled back to the stairs, when suddenly the floor gave a gigantic heave and there was the most deafening explosion which seemed to erupt from the bowels of the earth and rend the house apart at the joints. Sharonne clung frenziedly to the balusters, cowering into them with her head lowered in an effort to shield it from the *débris* which rained about her ears, whilst she implored heaven to save her.

When the terrifying noise of crashing timber and stone had died down she dared to glance up—appalled to see the entire east wing utterly demolished! 'Oh, Gabriel!' she gasped inwardly, for if he had been somewhere at that end of the house all would now indeed be lost.

The staircase seemed also about to give way as she descended cautiously, clutching her petticoats around her legs to evade the tongues of fire whilst hanging on to the right-hand banister—for the left side was completely ablaze—her eyes stinging, blinded by tears, though whether due to smoke or sheer wretchedness would be impossible to say. On she came, coughing and choking, her throat so raw and swollen she could scarely draw breath and when she did so the ebullient heat seared her lungs.

But even at this advanced hour she had not quite abandoned hope and her blurred vision strove continually to pierce the engulfing smoke, when she spied—in what had once been the library—something which made her rub her streaming eye and look again, trying to discern the object through her misery and the haze of dust and smoke. Reaching the bottom of the stairs, she stumbled closer to the distinctly white object . . . to discover it was a head! A white head—attached to a body lying prone beneath a veritable mountain of bricks and rubble. Oh, no—i-it couldn't be . . . not Gabriel?

With a cry which seemed to tear out her very heart, Sharonne threw herself down prostrate by the body—yes, it was *his* body. There was his white hair protruding from the mess of timber, broken glass and plaster.

Oblivious to the flames leaping about her, she grovelled wild at the *débris* covering him, sobbing hysterically, until her hands were cut and bleeding and her body ached with exhaustion. But on she battled, coughing spluttering, determined to free him though it was painfully obvious that he was quite beyond all human aid.

"G-Gabriel!" she choked pitifully. "S-Speak to m-me . . . tell m-me . . . y-you're alive!"

Alas, there was neither sound nor movement except for the interminable crackling and roaring of the fire as it continued to rage around her, growing perilously nearer and nearer, but still she did not relinquish her fight to rescue him and grappled with chunks of stucco plasterwork, torn books and dirt, screaming and sobbing until a human form eventually emerged outstretched, face down in the dust.

"Oh, Gabriel . . . y-you can't die! . . . I—won't let you . . . die!" She was seized by a coughing fit and she broke off, raising a grimy hand to her scorched face upon which the tears were drying as fast as she shed them, then began tugging and heaving to free the body, but all to no avail, for his sheer weight was quite beyond the capabilities of her shattered frame, and in a fit of despair she threw herself across him with a cry of agony.

"I l-loved you . . . G-Gabriel, and y-you never . . . even knew it . . . y-you were . . . the man I wanted! . . . I know I should still h-hate . . . y-you but I c-can't . . . I c-can't. . . ."

Again she lapsed into body-racking coughs, and as she glanced up and about all she could see was a blanket of fire leaping and dancing around her and the body at her side. Fingers of flame reaching out for her, beckoning her to join them in their frolic, mocking and jeering at her—and she could hear laughter! A man's strident laughter, the laughter of Lord Edmund St Claire, scoffing, gloating, that he was now Marquess of Ashton! Yes, it was all exactly as she had dreamed, of Edmund all in red doing the devil's dance. She could actually hear him, see him in the flames as they leapt higher and higher, growing hotter and hotter in their *danse macabre*.

'Sharonne! Sharonne!' she could hear them calling, the flames, Edmund—and Gabriel too, as in the dream. She could even hear the agony in his voice, see him reaching out to her. Yes, there were his scarred hands and his beautiful face—'No! No! Not his face!'—were her final words before she fell with an asphyxiating sob across the corpse, unconscious.

10

HEARING was the first of Sharonne's senses to respond to consciousness, and the sound of a peculiar rasping close at hand as if someone were sawing wood, but as she was luxuriating in the creature comfort of a warm cosy bed, presumably situated in the confines of a bedchamber, she was unable to give credence to her ears.

As she held her breath, the noise suddenly ceased, and she realised with a jolt that it was nought but the sound of her own breathing. Her poor lungs were protesting in the only way they knew—with loud raucous wheezes following their dreadful ordeal in the fire.

The fire! That one word flung wide her memory gates to the whole tragic occurrence, prompting her to wonder if she were alive or dead, in heaven or the other place—and Gabriel, where was he? She struggled to raise her eyelids, but they seemed to be as heavy as lead. And every time she tried to swallow, a thousand swords pierced her throat!

But all at once there was another sound, the soft whisper of petticoats, before something cold and moist contacted her burning forehead, ever so gently, then her flaming cheeks. Yes, she was undoubtedly in heaven, she sighed, wallowing in the rapture of it as she tried once again to open her eyes to gaze upon this unknown benefactor, when someone—apparently the benefactor—emitted a sharp gasp.

"Saints be praised!" exclaimed a woman's excited

voice within inches of her right ear. "I do declare, the young mistress be awakenin' at last!"

Northumberland House! Yes, that was where she was, now that she recalled. She had been presented to the Marquess of Ashton and fainted outright, but she could not reconcile the voice with that of my Lady Benton.

The rustling petticoats were heard to adjourn to the other side of the room where a door opened and the voice faded away declaring its earnest intention of informing the Marquess immediately, interlarded with further praises to the saints.

The female in question had barely disappeared when Sharonne's eyes finally opened. The lattice gaily hung with chintz was first to claim her attention, evoking a frown of some confusion.

'Chintz?' she asked herself. 'At Northumberland House?'

From the window her puzzled gaze travelled slowly round the modest room, over the low-beamed ceiling, the whitewashed walls to the homely fireplace wherein logs blazed merrily on this chill September day. Definitely not Northumberland House, nor Court St Claire for that matter. No, how could it be the Marquess's home when it was gone? All gone! Razed to the ground in that terrible inferno—and the Marquess gone with it.

'Oh, no, no! Not Gabriel! He couldn't be gone, lost to her for ever!'

A dry sob racked her feeble frame and she tried to cry, wanted desperately to cry, yet could not produce a single tear. All she could manage was a toad-like croak which rent her vocal chords asunder. But what of Edmund? Had he driven off to London without her?

Yes, yes, how she hoped this were indeed so, for he had never truly loved her, nor she him, and he was the last person she now wanted to see. He was cruel, abominably cruel! More so than Gabriel at his worst moment, when he had struck down Jonathan. Nevertheless, he had achieved his objective, for he, Edmund, would now be Marquess, with nothing or no one to stand in his way. Everything now belonged to him, all his brother's estate and wealth, everything but she herself, for she would never belong to him—never! But wait! Had not the woman said something about fetching the Marquess? No! No! Not Edmund! She could never face him again! She must get out of this house at all cost, away from Edmund and his vile wickedness. She could never face a lifetime in bondage to the man who had so heinously murdered the man she loved. She would as lief slave as the lowliest menial in bondage to honest folk rather than languish in luxury with *him*. There was no alternative, she must leave now whilst she had this opportunity.

Without pausing to consider whither she would run or even if she had strength enough to do so, she dragged herself up to sit clutching her head which cried out—along with every muscle in her aching body—in protest at this unexpected exertion. As she was clad in nought but a night-gown, her immediate problem was something to wear. Clothes, where were her clothes? Unknown to Sharonne, her hostess had considered these fit only to be destroyed, for they had been so badly charred in the fire. Nevertheless, Sharonne recognised the huge trunk before the fireplace wherein were packed her effects for her protracted journey to London. If she could only manage to reach it in time. . . .

She gained the edge of the bed and gingerly lowered her feet to the floor, then stood up, very, very cautiously. Yes, all was well so far, her legs were much stronger than she had anticipated.

But before she could venture a step her blood congealed as she detected the woman's footstep on the stair, heralding her return—no doubt, with the Marquess! It was too late, there was nothing she could do! She did not even have time to climb back into bed before the door swung open and a stout motherly body attired in brown homespun, white apron and matching frilled mop-cap contrasting vividly but not unattractively with her rosy visage, stood almost wedged in the doorway.

"Saints a-mercy!" she shrieked in alarm at sight of her charge swaying by the bedside, clutching once again at her revolving head. "Child! Child! Whatever are you adoin' out o' your bed?" she cried, hastening across the creaking floorboards. "Now then, what should 'is lordship say if 'e were to see you loik this? He be acomin' up surely just as soon as 'e's able, so you'd best be gettin' back into—"

"No! P-Please, I—I beg you, good dame, to help me!" pleaded Sharonne, grabbing at the other's plump dimpled arm. "I—I can't see him! I don't want to see him! I—"

"Dearie me, what koind o' talk's this? Don't want to see 'e?" ejaculated the dame, who bore a delicious aroma of home-baked bread about her ample person. "There, there now, little one," she cooed consolingly, enfolding Sharonne to her full-blown bosom as she might her own daughter. "That be no way to speak o' the man who wants to marry you."

"No, I c-can't marry him," she faltered, her throat hoarse, burying her burning face in the white cambric apron. "Y-You don't understand, I—I must get away before he comes. Oh, please, help me to get out of here, to escape his wrath, ma'am! Please t-take me to friends, relations, neighbours, anyone! Only please get me away before he kills me too! Y-You don't know the terrible thing he's d-done. . . ."

She broke off, sobbing in dire distress, her tears flowing at last, unaware that the good dame was hearkening to her desperate plea with but half an ear, for her attention was suddenly focused over the top of Sharonne's bowed golden head upon a third person, who stood by the door absorbing the scene in silence, a forefinger to his lips cautioning the dame to maintain the deception of his presence as he listened intently to Sharonne's entreaty.

"H-He's w-wicked, wicked! He drugged G-Gabriel . . . the true Marquess . . . and when he lay unconscious, he set the house afire. He burnt Gabriel alive, his own brother! I—I found his . . . I l-loved him so. . . . Oh, Gabriel . . . Gabriel. . . ." She sobbed anew, so distressed that she failed to notice the subtle exchange as the gentleman assumed the place of the good dame, who curtsied respectfully and tip-toed softly away, her rosy cheeks beaming in beautiful approval that all would be well ere her next batch of cottage loaves emerged from the oven.

"I t-tried to s-save him . . . oh, how I t-tried, but it was all no use . . . h-he was d-dead . . . quite, quite—"

She broke off in sudden bewilderment, remarking something passing strange, that although her scorched face still drew comfort from the feel of the smooth cambric, it was not the cambric of an apron but of a ruffled shirt. Furthermore, what lay beneath it was certainly not the plump bosom of the good dame but the sinewy chest of—a man! And the arms, slender yet vibrant with rippling muscle as they encompassed her form, arms she had felt thus before, yet which now seemed so long, long ago . . . that familiar body next to her own . . . that blissful touch of the long sensitive fingers under her chin, raising her face gently but firmly to receive his kiss, a kiss so infinitely tender at first as he nurtured her lips lingeringly beneath his own, waxing in intensity until he was devouring her in passionate abandon, straining her to him with a craving as desperate as her own. And though Sharonne could sense every bone in her body creaking as if about to disintegrate 'neath the pressure of his arms, and she almost cried out with the pain of it, she nevertheless could have cried out equally loudly in wildest joy, and would have just as eagerly volunteered to brave a dozen such fires as Court St Claire to experience another moment like this. . . .

"Gabriel! Gabriel! Y-You're alive!" she gasped and choked all at once, blinking away the tears from her hazel eyes to gaze up into his ardent blue. "I can't believe it, I truly can't! Y-You were dead, quite, quite dead!—I saw you with my own eyes!"

Gabriel St Claire, fourth Marquess of Ashton, emitted a crucifying groan and buried his face in the haven of her long auburn tresses, his arms enveloping her even tighter.

"Oh, Sharonne, Sharonne," he murmured in anguish. "Surely the agony I have borne throughout the past days, weeks, amply recompenses all the wrong I have

210

done you? Can you appreciate the hell I've endured whilst you lay here unconscious? And watching you and Edmund together, seeing you languishing in his arms when you should have been in mine? By the faith, no man breathing could have loved you as I loved you, and love you now! You are the angel, Sharonne, not I. You have wrought miracle upon miracle in me; you have proved my salvation out of all the women I've known; you have redeemed my soul from the depths of degradation by opening mine eyes to mine own iniquities and making me suffer as I in turn made others suffer, not least of all your dear brother, your parents, and yourself . . . yet you choose to love me, and perform the greatest miracle of all."

Again his lips sought hers in a further burst of passion, as if he were unable to credit this wonder and needed desperately to confirm it anew every few seconds by the pressure of her lips on his, the feverish grasp of her arms, fingers, about his neck, as she sacrificed every breath of adoration in her being to assuage his dire craving.

"No, Gabriel," breathed Sharonne at last, touching his fair hair, his pale cheek, his lips with her delicate fingers, as if seeking to reassure herself that it was really he, "the greatest miracle of all is that you are here with me, able to love me thus, for you were dead, I swear, though I tried everything humanly possible to save you."

"No, Sharonne. It was Edmund you saw and Edmund you tried to save."

"Edmund!" she exclaimed, aghast, drawing back in his arms to stare up at him askance. "B-But his hair, it was white! I saw it quite distinctly!"

The Marquess smiled to himself. "I've no doubt yours would be too, my own, if you had been felled to the floor with a stucco ceiling."

Sharonne giggled, a giggle nonetheless infected with a degree of hysteria, for her poor brain was being hard pressed to acknowledge the events which had come to pass.

"And to think that I was actually battling to save your wretched brother, Gabriel, indeed, almost sacrificed my life for him—and following his appalling act of burning down your lovely home, furthermore, with you in it!"

My lord cast her a downward cryptic glance. "Was I, Sharonne?" he parried enigmatically.

She returned a look of innocent enquiry. "Weren't you, Gabriel? May I ask exactly where you *did* choose to secrete yourself?"

"Perchance, during the night you overheard us quarrelling?" he deftly evaded the question.

"Yes. I heard shouting, but could not distinguish the topic of dispute."

"Mayhap that is as well, my love, for it was your own delectable self."

"Me? Y-You and Edmund were fighting over me?"

The Marquess nodded gravely. "He knew I loved you, wanted you, more than anything in the world. Yet when I begged him to release you from your obligation he refused, despite the fact that he—" He pulled up short, gnawing his lip in some dilemma and looking shamefaced.

"You may say what you wish, Gabriel," she enlightened him frankly. "I am well aware of your brother's true feeling towards me."

212

"He assured me that nothing on earth would sway him from his determination to wed you and flaunt you before mine eyes at every conceivable opportunity."

Sharonne could scarcely own herself surprised, for this was typical of Edmund.

"A-And then?" she prompted, agog.

"Had I been the man I was seven years ago I should have gone for my sword without a second thought. But something stayed me—no, not merely my present weakness, something more profound, call it conscience if you will, and I realised that bloodshed was not the answer. And so, after consuming Edmund's rather potent brew I did not retire to my chamber as he expected. Instead, I . . . I . . . ."

"Yes, Gabriel?"

"I went to—would you believe, my chapel?" He gave licence to an ironic laugh. "Forsooth, what would my friend Ravenby think to hear of my devotions thus?"

"Y-You prayed, Gabriel?" whispered she in awe, obviously impressed.

"Aye, I made a valiant attempt, though I had quite lost the intelligence of it," he confessed ruefully. "I was wont to regard it as a symptom of moral weakness, an evasion of life's adversities. And as I invariably preferred to dispense mine own justice and shape mine own destiny, I never found the need for such . . . until that night, when I suddenly appreciated that you were going out of my life and there was nothing I could do to prevent it—though I most certainly should have done something, anything, had I known how you truly felt!" His eyes deviated about the room, unable to meet her gaze. "It cost me dearly in pride and self-respect,

213

Sharonne, to admit I needed outside help. Nevertheless, I betook me to the chapel with my worthy valet—"

"Your man? He's safe?"

"Indeed. I struggled through two lines of my pathetic little imprecation when Edmund's wine took its toll and I passed into oblivion upon the altar steps. There I remained with my faithful James watching over my recumbent body until he spied fire belching from the house and made a strenuous effort to waken me. He eventually met with success. I immediately despatched him on horse to rouse the village whilst I braved the flames. I might not have ventured to do so had not the coach and six still been at the door, when I realised you had not left for London."

"A-And you found me, Gabriel? Y-You rescued me?"

"When I arrived on the scene there wasn't a great deal of the house left to search. There you were, conveniently positioned a few yards from the door but completely surrounded by flames. I could see you, hear you, but knew not how to approach you. I shouted myself hoarse but your ears were deaf to my entreaties as you lamented over Edmund's corpse, assuming it to be mine."

"Y-You actually ventured into the fire . . . to s-save me?" she breathed, her eyes shining up into his in ardent admiration.

"I could see nought else for it! If you were to go up in flames, then there wasn't much purpose in my surviving alone," he informed her candidly.

"Oh, Gabriel!" she whispered in rapture. "You risked your very life for me?"

"Did you not risk the same for me, Sharonne?" he parried softly.

She blushed, conscious of his passionate gaze—when she caught sight of his right hand swathed in bandages.

"M-My lord, y-your hand!" she burst out in concern, which he gestured aside.

"It will heal completely in a week or two, according to my physician. No, my love, what you must answer for is my hair! I swear on oath that there is not another female on God's good earth for whom I'd have willingly sacrificed six inches off my hair. Make no mistake, I shall extort a handsome price!"

Howbeit, though he endeavoured to distract her from the worst of his injuries with this light repartee, before he could stop her, Sharonne had raised a hand to his hair—now merely shoulder length—and exposed an ugly searing scar down his right cheek.

"G-Gab . . . ri . . . el," she gasped in bitter anguish, instantly comprehending the spiritual as well as physical pain this must have cost him.

"That too will disappear in time, my physician assures me," he endeavoured to make light of it, "though either way, 'tis a small price to pay for what was at stake," he appended, his smouldering eyes conveying much, much more as he raised her blistered fingers to his lips.

"Oh, my lord," she choked emotionally, throwing her arms around him. "Oh, Gabriel, how I do love you!"

The Marquess enfolded her to his heart, resting his scarred cheek upon her head.

"We make a sorry pair, do we not, Sharonne?" he sighed into her ear. "Do not you agree it high time we called a truce before one of us sustains some permanent injury?"

Sharonne could not have been in more wholehearted agreement. "Seven years is a long time to bear enmity," she observed philosophically.

"Aye," pondered my lord, gazing abstractedly at an embroidered text upon the wall exhorting all and sundry to love one another. "Ever since that mortal duel —though I persist in my defence, Sharonne, that my intention was simply to teach your brother a lesson he badly needed. Apart from which, it never occurred to me for a moment that you, a mere child, would have the unmitigated impudence to seek revenge where no man had ever dared. However, you got your revenge, did you not?"

"For which, I believe, I handsomely atoned with the mock marriage," she challenged impishly.

"Ah, not quite, my love," he mildly rebuked her. "If you recall, at the crucial hour I forsook my vengeance. Whate'er transpired 'pon the subsequent night was *not* in the cause of vengeance, of which you are abundantly aware."

A long significant pause greeted this admission as Sharonne fought nobly to meet her lord's eye but failed lamentably, he already anticipating the question hovering on her lips and wondering if she would rally sufficient courage to ask it.

"G-Gab . . . riel . . . ?" she murmured coyly, tracing an imaginary monogram upon his left shoulder with a forefinger. "I-If Edmund . . . had not arrived w-when he did . . . w-would you—er—I—I mean, d-did you . . . actually intend . . . to . . . to . . . er . . . ?"

216

He flashed her a disarming smile. "And what would you have me respond, my sweet Sharonne? For should I answer no, I did not so intend, you would scarce believe me. And if I were to answer yes, I should sink even lower in your valued esteem—should I not?"

The Marquess threw her a sidelong look of enquiry as she stood tongue-tied before him, nervously twining her fingers in her long hair.

"I pray you will not overlook the fact, dearest one, that a new-found emotion had but just struck me with all the delicacy of a twelve-pound cannon-ball. Faith, I am but mere mortal."

Sharonne bit her lip, giggled and flushed furiously, in that order, suddenly acutely conscious of her state of dishabille.

"Indeed, I should not hesitate to crave your forgiveness but for the crucifying agony you inflicted upon me afterwards when you revelled in Edmund's company from dawn unto dusk! I swear, 'twas the most execrable suffering I have ever endured, including my miserable years as the Sultan's favourite!"

"Is that why you were suddenly ill, Gabriel?" she probed curiously.

"I was *not* ill!" he objected emphatically.

"—merely indisposed," she completed without the vestige of a smile.

He elevated a reproving eyebrow. "Which brings us precisely where?"

"Two revenges to my credit, my Lord Marquess, and one to you—ere—if we are not to account the wedding night."

My lord could not forgo an infectious chuckle. "Furthermore, young lady, if nought else this ultimate saving of your neck must surely exonerate me in some measure from my former transgressions?"

Sharonne stretched up on her toes and kissed his scarred cheek.

"Yes, Gabriel," she whispered fervently. "I forgive you everything, but, alas, it leaves me sorely in your debt, a debt I know not how to repay."

He hesitated, debating within himself before venturing quietly, almost as if he did not wish her to hear: "You might discharge it in full with your own adorable self—a truly extortionate price, for I am not an easy man to live with."

She fixed him with a provocative eye, feigning surprise.

"I-Is this a proposal of marriage, Lord Ashton?"

"It is, Miss Falconer," winced the Marquess.

"*Another*, my lord?"

"Another!" he retorted, losing patience. "Confound you, woman, this time it's genuine! Quite, quite genuine! Pay heed—I have proof."

His lordship released her to delve inside his ruffled shirt and produce a folded document which he bestowed into her astonished hands.

"W-What is it, Gabriel?" she breathed apprehensively, unfolding it with care, to be confronted with a lengthy composition of legal and ecclesiastical jargon.

" 'Tis a licence, my love, permitting us to dispense with the tedious formality of lawful procedure and marry forthwith."

"And it is quite legitimate?"

"Zounds! O' course it is, ye sceptical wench," he rallied her as if she had no cause to be. "Was not Mr Walpole's own niece wed in like manner? And see, 'tis

218

endorsed by the Archbishop of Canterbury himself! Nonetheless," he went on, tongue-in-cheek, "if you are loath to trust me, we do have the alternative of a great elaborate conventional affair in London with half the world looking on, but which, alas, is absolutely out of the question until the full period of mourning for the passing of dear Edmund is quite expired."

"Oh, no, Gabriel!" she burst forth in ardent protest, to the Marquess's immense satisfaction. "I couldn't possibly wait all that time. H-How soon may be be wed w-with this licence?"

My lord beamed his approval. "As soon as you consider yourself well enough to—er—"

"Resume from your brother's timely intrusion?" she concluded in wide-eyed innocence.

A peculiar cough erupted from my lord. "Well—er—yes, an ye so wish, dear heart," he recovered himself on the instant. "Forsooth, I'll send for Parson Pendlebury to unite us this very afternoon!"

Sharonne dimpled up at him sweetly. "This afternoon should suit very nicely, thank you, my lord," she approved demurely. "And I should be further obliged if you would be good enough to tell me exactly where we are."

The Marquess returned a blank stare. "You did not recognise Mrs Guthrie, the lodge-keeper's wife?"

"Should I, when I have seen her no more than twice —and that from the back of a horse?" returned Sharonne pleasantly.

"She and I have sat turn about at your bedside throughout the last two days—"

"Two days! I have actually lain here at your lodge for two whole days?"

" 'Pon honour, considering the wild delirium you labour'd 'neath, two whole weeks would not have surprised me."

"Delirium, Gabriel " queried she dubiously, again recalling her fantastic nightmares. "D-Did I say anything which m-might be misconstrued, or cause embarrassment?"

My lord favoured her with his rare angelic smile. "You merely left no one in any doubt about your feelings for me."

The blood rushed to her cheeks. "Oh, Gabriel! However shall I face Mr and Mrs Guthrie?"

"My love, ere the day is through, alas, you will be obliged to face more than Mr and Mrs Guthrie," he enlightened her, taking her arm to guide her over to the casement which he flung wide. "Look yonder."

Sharonne followed his indication way across the verdant pastures of his estate to some kind of building set high on a hill not too far away. Close enough, in fact, for her to distinguish the people hastening to and fro—indeed, the whole scene buzzed with activity.

"My tenants, Sharonne," he announced on a note of unmistakable pride. "Do not they delight one's heart? They returned with James a trifle too late to extinguish the fire, and so for the past days have rallied to the cause of setting the Dower House into habitable order —it will be ready tonight. Do observe how even my Squire and his good family ably assist in the operation."

"You must feel justly proud of them, Gabriel," Sharonne declared, quite overcome. "We must arrange some kind of celebration in their honour, to repay their kindness."

"Aye," sighed his lordship ruefully. "I protest, they put me to the blush, for I have long neglected them. Methinks 'tis high time I rectified the oversight and sought to make restitution." He cast her a downward meaningful look. "Speaking of restitution, dear one, I give you my word, on sworn oath, that I shall do all that is humanly possible to reconcile you with your parents. Obviously," he hastened to add, "they will never forgive me. No, Sharonne," he silenced her attempt to remonstrate, "I cannot expect it, and never shall! However, some day when we present them with a grandson, perchance it will compensate in some small measure . . . for the son . . . they . . . lost."

Her gaze lingered a while longer on the industrious little scene before it wandered away to the left, as if drawn by some strange sinister instinct, to the desolate blackened ruin which, only three days previous, had been the impressive home of the St Claire family. And despite all the tragedy and unhappiness embraced therein, Sharonne could not prevent a tear welling in her eye and trickling slowly down her cheek—which did not go unremarked by her lord, who took her tenderly in his arms, drawing her head to rest on his firm shoulder.

"Fret not, my sweet life," he whispered, choked with emotion. "Mayhap I shall commission that new Adam fellow to rebuild it in the Italian style—they do say he is rapidly becoming the rage." He heaved a tremendous sigh, planting a kiss upon her golden hair. " 'Tis of some consolation to know that 'twas not sacrificed in vain."

"No, Gabriel," she agreed, smiling through the film

of tears. "Neither was Jonathan. Good has emerged from all the unhappiness, has it not, my lord? . . . Our love!"

And as the future Marchioness of Ashton gazed up, her beautiful eyes cherishing passionate promise for the night ahead, my Lord Marquess was forced to acquiesce.

Mary Stewart

"Mary Stewart is magic" is the way Anthony Boucher puts it. Each and every one of her novels is a kind of enchantment, a spellbinding experience that has won acclaim from the critics, millions of fans, and a permanent place at the top.

☐ AIRS ABOVE THE GROUND	23868-7	$1.95
☐ THE CRYSTAL CAVE	23315-4	$1.95
☐ THE GABRIEL HOUNDS	23946-2	$1.95
☐ THE HOLLOW HILLS	23316-2	$1.95
☐ THE IVY TREE	23251-4	$1.75
☐ MADAM, WILL YOU TALK	23250-6	$1.75
☐ THE MOON-SPINNERS	23941-4	$1.95
☐ MY BROTHER MICHAEL	22974-2	$1.75
☐ NINE COACHES WAITING	23121-6	$1.75
☐ THIS ROUGH MAGIC	22846-0	$1.75
☐ THUNDER ON THE RIGHT	23940-3	$1.95
☐ TOUCH NOT THE CAT	23201-8	$1.95

Buy them at your local bookstores or use this handy coupon for ordering:

FAWCETT BOOKS GROUP
P.O. Box C730, 524 Myrtle Ave., Pratt Station, Brooklyn, N.Y. 11205

Please send me the books I have checked above. Orders for less than 5 books must include 75¢ for the first book and 25¢ for each additional book to cover mailing and handling. I enclose $_____ in check or money order.

Name_____
Address_____
City_____ State/Zip_____

Please allow 4 to 5 weeks for delivery.

B-1